"Let me show you my lair," Con insisted. "It's all done in wolf and tiger pelts."

Heller smiled at his teasing words, but her eyes were shining. "How fitting," she said tartly, but shaky laughter bubbled through her lips.

Con lifted her hand to his lips, nibbling gently on her fingers, then turning her hand to press a hot kiss into her palm. "My brave heroine," he murmured, dropping kisses along the delicate skin of her wrist and arm.

Her cheeks reddened with pleasure and more than a little heat, while her eyes glowed like newly mined turquoise.

"You have such power," Con said huskily, then pulled her against him with a suddenness that made Heller gasp softly.

"I can't promise you forever, Con. Please don't talk about commitment."

"For now," he said, "let's just talk of love." His mouth was so close to hers that each word was a whispered embrace, a caress on her lips that enflamed her.

"Touch me, Con," she begged. "Touch me now . . ."

WHAT ARE *LOVESWEPT* ROMANCES?

They are stories of true romance and touching emotion. We believe those two very important ingredients are constants in our highly sensual and very believable stories in the *LOVESWEPT* line. Our goal is to give you, the reader, stories of consistently high quality that may sometimes make you laugh, sometimes make you cry, but are always fresh and creative and contain many delightful surprises within their pages.

Most romance fans read an enormous number of books. Those they truly love, they keep. Others may be traded with friends and soon forgotten. We hope that each *LOVESWEPT* romance will be a treasure—a "keeper." We will always try to publish

LOVE STORIES YOU'LL NEVER FORGET
BY AUTHORS YOU'LL ALWAYS REMEMBER

The Editors

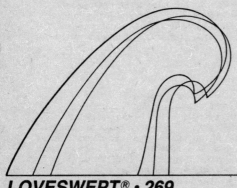

LOVESWEPT® • 269

Helen Mittermeyer
Ablaze

BANTAM BOOKS
TORONTO · NEW YORK · LONDON · SYDNEY · AUCKLAND

ABLAZE

A Bantam Book / July 1988

*LOVESWEPT® and the wave device are registered
trademarks of Bantam Books, a division of Bantam
Doubleday Dell Publishing Group, Inc. Registered in
U.S. Patent and Trademark Office and elsewhere.*

*If you would be interested in receiving protective vinyl
covers for your Loveswept books, please write to this address
for information:*

*Loveswept
Bantam Books
P.O. Box 985
Hicksville, NY 11802*

ISBN 0-553-21892-1

Published simultaneously in the United States and Canada

*Bantam Books are published by Bantam Books, a division
of Bantam Doubleday Dell Publishing Group, Inc. Its trademark, consisting of the words "Bantam Books" and the
portrayal of a rooster, is Registered in U.S. Patent and
Trademark Office and in other countries. Marca Registrada.
Bantam Books, 666 Fifth Avenue, New York, New York 10103.*

PRINTED IN THE UNITED STATES OF AMERICA

O   0 9 8 7 6 5 4 3 2 1

One

Con Wendel was bored and irritated and hiding out in the bar of one of the hotels his family owned. Wendel International had its fingers in many pies, not the least of which were fifteen gold-star hotels throughout the world. Con's earlier plan to dine and reminisce with his two closest friends, Pacer Dillon and Dev Abrams, had backfired. Pacer was out of town and Dev was reviewing a new play on Broadway.

Damn! He was in town on business and had felt the need of men, the uncomplicated, easy friendship he had with the two who'd shared Princeton and Vietnam with him. He was sick of the scene, the glitz, the pomp, the pretense that went with his position of wealth and family.

The Andre Manhattan on Park Avenue was a quietly opulent hotel that had been shrewdly run by the same staff for the last fifteen years. For Con, the hotel's greatest asset at the moment was that no one there knew him. Bela Petronides, the manager, was the only person who might have recognized him, and he was at a conference in Barbados with the other managers of the Wendel hotels.

Con moodily sipped his Irish whiskey and branch water and stared again at one of the cocktail waitresses. For several minutes he'd been admiring her shapely figure and the speed with which she did her job. She seemed to move twice as fast as the two other waitresses. There was a tenseness, almost a desperation about her that intrigued him. The multitude of interesting things New York City could offer had no pull for him this Friday night, but the waitress was a welcome diversion. Again and again he stared at her.

He noticed that she counted her tip each time she picked one up. Sometimes she was pleased, other times she grimaced. Money was important to the tall full-figured blonde. As he admired her fabulous legs beneath the short black skirt of her uniform, Con felt desire curl inside him.

Five minutes later he finished his drink, threw some money on the table, and walked slowly across the room to a booth he knew the voluptuous blonde tended. In less than a minute she was standing beside him. "Hello," he said, smiling up at her. "I was wondering if I could get something to eat."

She cocked her head, her eyes sliding sideways. "Weren't you just at another table?"

Con was stunned by the warm feeling that suffused him because she'd noticed him earlier. "I was."

She looked unsure for a moment, then shrugged. "I suppose it's not up to me if a customer wants to change seats."

"True." Now that she was close, he could see that her eyes were a magnificent turquoise and, despite her makeup, that her skin had a translucent purity to it.

"The kitchen is still open," she said, "but not for much. I could get you a sandwich, maybe a salad. They do a great shrimp pocket sandwich here and I'd make sure the greens were very fresh. How does that sound?"

"Great," he said. When she hesitated, he raised his brows inquiringly. "What's wrong?"

"Nothing. I hope there was no problem at the other table, sir."

"Everything is fine, but I am hungry."

"Coming right up."

As she scampered away, Con had a very good view of her derriere in the tight skirt. Very nice! Rounded, full, luscious. Getting to know the golden blonde was becoming imperative.

He was still watching her, when his former waitress accosted her. Her kissable mouth tightened, her small but firm chin jutted forward. It would seem she could handle herself.

"Lock, Sandy, I did not take the customer away from you. He changed tables on his own."

"Don't tell me you weren't eyeing that hunk, Heller, because I saw you."

"I haven't time to argue with you. Did you get a tip?"

"Yes, but—"

"Then you should stop complaining. Excuse me, I have orders to get."

Heller did feel a pinch of guilt. She hadn't tried to coax the "hunk" to one of her tables, but she sure had noticed him. Tall and broad-shouldered, he had dark brown hair that glinted with reddish high-lights. And his deep green eyes had seemed to pierce her when he'd spoken to her. At close range she'd even noticed the golden rays in them.

She'd been startled when he'd sat at one of her tables but wasn't going to dwell on his possible rea-sons for moving. With a little luck he might leave a good tip. That was all she wanted. She couldn't and wouldn't dwell on his overpowering sexuality. Her mother's illness was her greatest concern . . . and how to get the crucial ten thousand dollars for her bypass surgery was next on the list!

If only there were more time, if only she were in a position to get a loan. Her life was riddled with ifs, but somehow she had to get the money.

"Heller," the bartender called to her. "The bell rang. Your order is ready. Are you adding up your tips already?"

"Thanks, Pete." Heller smiled at the bartender. Pete knew she needed the money for a family prob-lem but no more than that. She shied away from closeness with other people. She'd learned that early, when she and her mother had had to go into hiding.

She expertly balanced the dishes on her tray, stud-ied the salad and sandwich critically, then wove her way across the room to the "hunk." "Sorry, sir," she said as she set the plates in front of him. "I didn't ask if you would like something to drink. Coffee, tea?"

"This is fine," Con said. "Have you eaten?" Just having her stand near him sent another surge of want through him.

"Me? Oh, no, sir. That is, I'll eat something later."

"Will you join me?"

She shook her head. "I can't do that. I'd lose my job." She started to turn away.

"Maybe we could discuss that."

She stopped and looked at him warily. "What does that mean?"

"It means I'd like to know when you're off tonight so that we could have a few drinks and talk."

"I see."

"I hope you do." He watched as myriad expressions flashed across her heart-shaped face. "Couldn't we just talk?"

"Yes, we can do that, but my shift doesn't end until one."

"Isn't that a little odd? I thought shifts in most hotels went from six until two."

She nodded. "They do, but I generally come in at noon every day. I have permission to work a double shift." All at once she looked uneasy, as though she'd said too much. "I have to go. If you're still here when I'm done, I suppose we could talk."

Con nodded, noting again that tension in her. Her entire body seemed as taut as a bow string. "You shouldn't work so hard," he said.

"Actually I feel better when I'm active." She sprinted away.

For the next hour and a half he watched her speed through her job . . . and watched other men gaze admiringly at her, even flirt with her. The spurt of possessive anger that shot through him at every other man's lustful glance surprised him. Why should he feel possessive of the blond waitress?

At one minute after one she deposited her tray on the bar and left the room. During the next ten minutes Con looked at his watch many times, his impatience unexpected and annoying.

When she appeared at his table, face scrubbed, hair hanging loose about her shoulders, and wearing a denim skirt, a matching jacket, and Reeboks, he rose to his feet slowly.

She smiled. "I can see by your face you were hoping for svelte and soignée. Instead, you're getting active and prepared. I usually walk to work or I run for the bus." She tipped her head to one side. "Let's call it a night, shall we? We'll both be more comfortable."

Con took hold of her arm. "It makes sense to wear Reeboks to chase a bus. Have you caught any?"

"Once or twice."

He caught his breath at her enchanting elfin grin and the dimple that appeared at the side of her mouth. "Tell me your name."

"Heller. And let's just stick to first names."

"Heller? Unusual. My name is Conrad. Con to my friends. What would you like to drink?"

"Saratoga water and lime, please."

Con gave the order, then sat down next to her on the banquette. "Tell me about yourself, Heller."

"Not much to tell. I'm from upstate New York, went to college there, but dropped out during my junior year."

"To be a cocktail waitress?"

"I guess you could say that."

Con was frustrated by her brief answers. Perhaps, he thought, if he talked about himself, she might unbend some. So during the next several minutes he told her about his growing up in Manhattan, being the head of a corporation, and his former hobby.

"You were really a race car driver?" she asked incredulously.

"Yes. I gave it up a few years ago. I had a minor accident with minimal injuries, but I decided I didn't want to push my luck." She seemed more at ease with him now, and he decided not to probe into her life. There would be time to do that when they were better acquainted.

When the bar closed they were both surprised.

"I don't want to take you home yet," he said.

"It's not necessary for you to take me home at all," she said as they walked out into the hotel lobby. "You could wait with me while I get a cab, though."

"I don't mind driving you."

"No thanks."

Heller had no intention of letting him near her home, an apartment owned by a friend in a renovated warehouse in the West Village near the Hudson River. Although she'd known Con only a few hours, already she felt a potent attraction to him. He was handsome and charming, and he had been sensitive enough not to pry into her life. She liked him for that. But more, shivers of sexual excitement had run through her every time his gaze had lingered on her, every time his hand or shoulder or thigh had brushed against her. She couldn't allow this man to get too close to her. It would be dangerous—for both of them.

"What are you thinking?" he asked suddenly.

Startled, she blinked, then realized that she'd been silent for a few minutes as she mulled over her attraction to Con. "Uh . . . I was thinking about my dog."

Dumbfounded, he stared at her. Comprehension dawned slowly, and she laughed.

"I bet you're not used to being supplanted by an animal," she said. Her laughter died away and she started toward the doors. "This has been nice, but I should get home. I have a long day tomorrow."

He followed her outside into the warm May night. The doorman flagged down a cab for her, and she turned to Con. "Thank you for a lovely evening," she said, holding out her hand.

He shook her hand but then didn't immediately release it. "You're very welcome, Heller," he said in a soft, intimate voice that made her tremble. "Same time tomorrow?"

"S-sure," she stammered. She pulled her hand free and hurried into the waiting cab.

Con watched until the cab had disappeared, heading south on Park Avenue. Heller's image remained with him through the night.

For the rest of the week Con returned to the bar every night to spend as much time as he could with Heller. She was increasingly more relaxed with him but still told him virtually nothing about herself, still insisted that he should not drive her home. He would have thought she didn't like him at all, wasn't the least bit interested in her, if he hadn't been aware of his effect on her.

Whenever he touched her, however lightly and casually, she would tense, but she wouldn't pull away. Sometimes he caught her staring at him, an intriguing expression of desire and sadness in her eyes. He sensed that she, like himself, wanted their friendship to bloom into something more, yet needed to hold back from him. Her constraint frustrated him.

On Saturday night, his fifth straight night in the bar, Con felt particularly frustrated. Not only was the place so crowded that all of Heller's tables were occupied and he had to sit at the bar, but he was returning to Chicago the next day. Already he had been away from his business too long, and there was an important meeting Monday morning that he could not miss. Before this evening ended, he vowed as he watched Heller flit past him, her tray loaded with drinks, that he would force their friendship to advance a few crucial steps.

"She really moves," he said to the bartender, nodding toward Heller.

Pete smiled. "She's a worker." His smile faded. "I guess she really needs the money. She told me her family is in some sort of a bind and she needs ten thousand dollars. That kind of money isn't easy to come by, even with good tips."

A customer signaled to Pete, and with a nod to Con he moved away. Con shifted on his stool so he could watch Heller.

Ten thousand dollars, he thought. What could she need that much money for? Ten thousand dollars was nothing to him, but to a cocktail waitress . . . He sipped his drink, wondering if there was some way he could help her out.

At closing time that night, Heller rose reluctantly from the booth she'd been sharing with Con. She wasn't going to see him again, since he was returning to Chicago, and that thought was astonishingly painful. This past week he had colored all her dreams, waking and sleeping, and every night she had waited eagerly for him to appear.

She knew her infatuation with him was ridiculous. Not only did she not have the time for a relationship with a man, even one as marvelous as Con, but it was obvious they were from different worlds. What place could a cocktail waitress have in the glamorous, sophisticated world of a wealthy corporate executive?

"Good-bye, Con," she said softly. "I've had a wonderful time."

He grabbed her hand. "Don't go. Come up to my suite with me. We can talk longer there."

Desire tore at her. She wanted to be with him so much! "Ah . . . No, I must leave."

"Just for a short time. You told me you don't have to work tomorrow."'

She hesitated for only a moment more. She shouldn't do this, but . . . "I can't stay long."

"Then let's go right now."

Insanity, she thought as he escorted her to the elevators. What if he were a mad rapist? What if he—no! Heller put her imagination on hold. She'd learned a great deal about Con these last few nights. She had even toyed with the idea of telling him of her mother's need for heart surgery, but hadn't succumbed. That could involve danger for her mother, even for Con. If only her father had survived the plane crash when he'd been returning from a symphony tour, things would have been different. He would have dealt with the threat of the Domini brothers. . . .

When the elevator doors closed behind them, she swallowed hard.

Con watched her as the elevator opened right into the foyer of the penthouse suite.

"It's very elegant," she said. "You must have quite an expense account."

He grinned. "I do all right." He walked down the few steps into the conversation pit. Flicking a few switches, he set the lights on low and started the compact disc player. Then he faced her. "Come sit

down and I'll order us some . . . seltzer water."
Warmth flooded through him as she smiled, flashing that dimple of hers again. "We'll talk, relax, maybe even dance."

He hadn't turned into a ravenous beast, Heller thought, and nodded with relief. "That sounds wonderful to me." Still, her fears that this evening would turn into more than simple conversation rose again. When he approached her, his arms outstretched, she took a step back, raising one hand, palm outward.

"What's wrong?" he asked.

"I get the feeling I'm about to step into an abyss."

His arms dropped. "Not too flattering."

"You could have paid someone to be flattering, but not me."

His hands balled into fists. "I never *pay*, lady."

She lifted her chin and took another step backward. "I've offended you. I'll leave. Sorry." She turned and strode toward the elevator.

"No!" Con grabbed her, his arms encircling her waist, pulling her back to him. "I seem to have a short fuse where you're concerned." The feel of her body against his made his blood race.

"Yes," she whispered.

Though she was by no means a thin woman, he could tell she was trim and firm. What would she look like nude? "I apologize," he said.

"So do I, for being so . . . snappish."

He turned her in his arms and looked down at her. "Stay with me. We'll start again."

She nodded.

Her eyes had turned a deep turquoise, setting him on fire. He stepped back from her a bit and took her hand, threading his fingers through hers. "Would you like to see the rest of the suite?"

"Yes. Could I use the bathroom, please?"

He pointed her toward an open doorway. "Take your choice. There's one on the second floor and one down here." He watched her go down the hall, then abruptly made a decision. He picked up the phone and dialed a number, then issued a few terse instructions to the man on the other end.

When Heller returned he had poured two glasses of seltzer water, added lime slices, and set them on a low coffee table. She stopped before she reached him to study a large painting of a downcast Indian seated on a woebegone horse.

"Heller? Heller, come back from the cloud you're on."

"This is the first original I've seen outside of a museum, Con."

"Is it?" He walked over to her. "There are many wonderful things I'd like to show you." Cupping her chin in his hand, he leaned down and pressed his lips to hers.

Heller's experience with men was not extensive. The only man she'd cared about had been one in college. She had had to sever their relationship completely when she and her mother had been relocated three years ago. Since then her fears that she would never be entirely safe had kept her from getting involved with anyone. But Con's sweet, all-encompassing kiss made her forget those fears. As if it were the most natural thing in the world, she parted her lips and let her tongue tangle with his.

"Darling! Don't." Con pushed back from her, his breathing harsh. "I don't think you understand how strong an effect you have on me."

"Well, yes, I do, because you have the same effect on me." She stroked the strong line of his jaw. "It's been a long time since I've let anyone kiss me like that."

A cocky smile cracked his face. "Really? I'm honored." He pulled her close, lowering his head so his mouth was close to her ear. "Does that mean," he whispered, "if it comes to that, you want me to take care of the precautions?"

She squeezed her eyes shut as his sensual voice seemed to melt her insides. "Please." Her heart thudded out of rhythm. Had she just committed herself to him sexually? Hadn't she been the wary one? He pulled back and stared down at her. His green eyes had turned to emerald fire.

"Do you mean it?"

The bell to the suite rang just then.

Con glared at the elevator, then dropped a kiss on her nose. "Keep the thought," he said, and stalked across the room, taking an envelope from a uniformed man who'd stepped out of the elevator. He walked with the envelope to the table and smiled at Heller. "Business," he said briefly.

"Oh." She turned and walked to the window to look out on the lighted Manhattan skyline. She was scarcely aware of the soft noises Con made.

Returning to her, he gently pulled her into his arms, turning her, then holding her loosely. As he gazed into her eyes, he began to sway in rhythm to the sweet music that emanated from every corner of the room. "Why don't we relax with each other and talk?"

"Wasn't that what we decided?" She was surprised by the faint tremor in her voice. What a bizarre evening!

"So it is." He pressed his mouth to her hair. "You move beautifully."

"I like to dance," she said, and smiled up at him.

For an instant his heart stopped beating. There was a swelling pain in his chest, as though he would burst if he couldn't care for and nurture this woman. He shook his head to clear it; he was demented. "Tell me more about yourself. What was your major in college before you had to leave?"

"Music and theater arts. My father wanted me to concentrate on classical music as he had, but I was much more interested in the theater. I worked in every production at the university, and I've been involved in summer stock almost every year since I was fifteen."

"Quite the performer," he murmured, intrigued by this glimpse of her life. With her statuesque figure and expressive face, he imagined she would have undeniable presence on the stage.

The music changed to a song with a faster tempo, and he swung her out from his body. She looked down and grimaced. "I think I should take off my sneakers if we're going to dance on these beautiful carpets. My employers wouldn't think it too wonderful that I was tromping on them like this."

"We'll both take off our shoes." He led her to a chair and sat her down. He removed both of her shoes, then cupped one ankle and kissed her toes, right through her white anklet.

"I—I hope you don't think I'm going to do that for you, Con."

"No, darling, you're going to dance with me." He laughed and kicked off his own shoes, then pulled her to her feet.

Heller loved the freedom of dancing in socks. But after a minute she stopped and removed them. "Barefoot is better."

"Right." Conrad looked down at her long but small-boned feet and his breathing became impeded. His heart thudded heavily. "Your feet are lovely . . . and very erotic."

"Foot fetish?"

"I think it just started."

"You're a silly man." She tapped him on the nose, wanting to laugh, to cry, to shout Con's name from the top of the Empire State Building. Why? What magic did this man have?

He pulled her close and they swayed to a love ballad, her arms linked around his neck, his tight about her waist.

The music changed again.

"Can you jitterbug, Con? My mother and father used to do this and they taught me." Gyrating freely to the fifties music, Heller lost the tiredness she usually felt after her long shift. The lively music seemed to enter her being and energize her. She was delighted when Con joined her.

Arms and legs moving madly, they didn't even slow until the song ended.

Laughing, they fell forward into each other's arms. Con easily pulled her down to the floor as amusement poured in waves from them.

"You're out of breath, my beautiful Heller."

"So are you." She fanned herself with one hand.

When Con took her hand and pressed it to his face, she didn't struggle. "You're warm too," she said.

"Very." He leaned over her and quickly kissed her, then rolled onto his back. She sat up, Indian fashion, careful to keep her body still touching his. "Tell me more about your parents," he said.

More, she wondered. What had she told him already? Her eyes slid to his, catching his gaze on her. "You have wonderful green eyes."

"And yours are beautiful and expressive turquoise eyes, Heller mine."

She should have been irritated at his possessive endearment, yet wasn't. "I feel very comfortable with you," she said.

"Don't sound so bewildered by it, darling." He lifted her hand and kissed the palm. "It feels very good for me too."

"I am surprised, though. Everything about you is a surprise. You seem to cut through things like an extra-sharp knife."

"Changing the subject? We were talking about us."

"Trying to keep things on keel."

"I'm feeling a little off balance myself."

She laughed. "You? Mr. Cool? Never."

He turned on to his side, propping his head up on one hand. With his other hand he took one of hers and placed it on his chest. "See? My heart's going like a freight train, but I'm still very relaxed with you."

"I'm glad." She leaned over him, studying him as though she would know every pore.

He moved his hand to the back of her head and pushed her hair forward, then he pulled her even closer. "I'd like a curtain around me. Do you mind?"

"No."

"Don't move away from me, Heller."

"I won't."

"Will you kiss me if I keep my hands where they are?"

She pressed her lips chastely against his, and a quiver ran through her at the impersonal gesture. "There."

"Thanks." Con felt he'd just experienced one of the most erotic moments of his life. Blood pounded through his body. He reached up one finger and touched her lips. "These are beautiful, Heller darling."

"Are they?" She kissed him, this time more firmly.

"Wonderful." And it was. Kissing Heller was more than the loving gesture it was meant to be. It was his destruction and rebirth all in one sensual rush. He was on fire for her. She'd torched him and set him ablaze.

"Is something wrong, Con? You just frowned." She dared to touch the corner of his mouth with her tongue. "You fascinate me."

"Good, because you're pulling me apart, Heller with no last name."

She let herself fall forward onto his chest, sighing in delight when his arms closed around her. "I don't think it's supposed to be this way. We talk too much, laugh, giggle. It's silly."

"Maybe this is the first time we've ever made love, Heller."

She chuckled. "Are you a virgin, Con?"

"I feel like one. This has never happened to me until this moment, Heller mine." He pulled her tighter to him, loving her breasts pressing against him.

A raw stillness fell suddenly, the unspoken question radiating like a tuning fork. Anticipation lay heavy in the air.

"There's all kinds of time to turn me down, Heller, but if you don't resist me now, I am going to make love to you." He kissed her, then slid down so that her breast, still clothed, was in his mouth.

The sucking sensation coursed through her like a flood of lava. Heller lifted her body slightly so that he had freer access to her. Clinging to him, she twined her fingers in his hair, holding him close. Every part of her was melting. When one of her legs fell between his and his thighs tightened around her, she felt as though she would burst.

Tentatively, she touched his neck, her fingers trying to slip beneath his collar.

He released her breast as he wrenched his tie away from his throat and popped off the top button of his shirt. "Touch me, darling."

"I want to, Con. So much." Hands shaking, she undid the rest of the buttons.

"Will you be warm here? Or shall we go up to the bed?"

"I'm plenty warm," she said, and lowered her head to kiss the hot silky skin of his chest.

With a muffled oath Con lifted her, rolling her onto her back. He stripped his trousers off with little regard for the expensive material, then naked, barely able to restrain himself, turned to her once more. "Now you, my little one."

"I'm not little." Her breathless voice was unrecognizable. Con eased her blouse off, and she groaned as he kissed her breasts again through the thin nylon of her bra. When he unfastened her skirt and slid it down over her hips, she almost apologized for her plain cotton five-and-dime-store underwear. He was probably used to women dressed in silk, but she didn't spend money on anything except her mother anymore.

"What is it, darling?" he asked, apparently seeing the expression of embarrassment on her face. "Am I too rough?"

He didn't care about her underthings, she thought, feeling foolish. "No, you're very gentle."

He helped her up into a kneeling position and

removed the rest of her clothes. Once more they were still, gazing at each other, in frank hunger, in sexual appraisal.

"You have wonderful breasts."

She reached out to him. "I like your chest and the arrow of hair here." Her finger scored down the center of his body, below his waist.

He groaned. "Darling. Please. Don't touch me for a moment."

"What's wrong?" She tried to back away from him, but he didn't release her.

"I feel like an inexperienced boy, and if you make one more erotic wiggle, the show may be over. Don't laugh, witch."

"I'm not. I'm being very still."

"It isn't helping."

As one they sank to the carpet again, lying on their sides, face-to-face.

"I don't think anything could tamp the fire you ignite in me, Heller. Your eyes are seductive enough to blow me apart."

"I'm glad." She had never felt such power. Leaning nearer, she nibbled at the corner of his mouth. "It's been so much fun. We must be doing something wrong."

"My darling, I assure you we're doing nothing wrong." He scooped her under him, and gently, with one smooth, easy thrust, he entered her. Immediately he was motionless, overwhelmed by the feeling of rightness that welled within him.

Heller sighed. "It does feel great, doesn't it?" She moved sinuously beneath him, and a volcano of ecstasy erupted within her. "Oh!" Passion billowed through her and she surged against him.

Con answered her movement with one of his own,

the mighty force capturing them and thrusting them over the brink into the maelstrom of rapturous love. Spinning, twisting, falling, limbs entwining, hearts beating together, they clutched each other and reached heaven as one.

"My goodness." Heller clung to him. "You should tell your company about that and bottle it."

He eased his body from hers and lay beside her. "We're not into miracles."

For several minutes they lay in still, contented silence, then Heller reached for her blouse. Con stopped her. "No, darling, don't put that on. I'll only have to remove it again." His lazy smile dared her to contradict him.

The world had stopped and started again. All evening the painful thought of being parted from Con had haunted her, but at least it didn't have to happen yet. They were going to make love again! Planets and stars had exploded like rockets of joy.

"That sounds like a good idea, Con." She idly traced circles on his chest with a finger. "You know, I've never been so comfortable naked in front of someone, except my college roommate."

"Ah, that puts me in my place. Just a friend."

She giggled, then stared when she saw an expression of rather pained surprise on his face. "What is it?"

"When you laughed your breasts moved against me. I'm going to be ready to love you again very soon."

"You can't!"

He nodded, then kissed her breasts. "This carpet will always have a warm spot for me."

"How many other people do you suppose have thought the same thing?"

"None." His growled reply made her smile. He rose to his feet and pulled her up with him, holding her close. "See? I want you again."

His velvet-hard arousal was pressed against her soft belly, and her knees went weak with desire. "I guess it's back to the carpet again." She laughed out loud when he caught her up in his arms and strode across the large room, out to the foyer, and up the stairs. "You are strong if you take the stairs two at a time carrying me."

"You're light as a feather, my darling, and please don't infer anything else from that. I love your body just as it is."

"If you say so." She pressed her mouth to his neck. He wasn't hers; she could not possess him. But for one short night he was, and she could.

In bed the love play was resumed. Again there was laughter and frolic between them.

"I can't believe this," Con told her, his face pressed between her breasts. "Making love with you is so exciting but so restful. I think I may be committed after making a statement like that."

"I feel the same way. It might sound perverse if we say it's like making love to a best friend."

He lifted his head, his eyes half-closed and glittering with passion. "But it's true. I may have to send us to camp this summer. Wouldn't that be fun?"

"Shame on you, Con. You're leering."

Their desire was fired again. They rolled on the huge round bed as though it were their personal playground. Passion groaned from them. Laughter joined it. Their wild, insane lovemaking brought them delight and created another world for them alone.

"Oh, God, Con, I think I love you."

"Don't sound so sad and surprised, darling. I feel the same, and believe me, it's a first."

Embracing each other, face-to-face, they fell asleep, their languorous bodies satiated and content.

Heller opened her eyes and knew it was night and that she wasn't in her own room. In milliseconds she remembered Con and that she loved him. Turning her head, she looked into that wonderful face and smiled. He was sleeping so deeply, it was as though he took a breath only every minute.

How long she lay in the warmth of his arms, loath to leave him, Heller wasn't sure, but reality crashed around her as images of her mother filled her mind. There was no getting away from reality for long.

Swinging her head back, Heller looked up into the darkness. Taking deep breaths, she calmed herself, buried the grief that was building in her because she was leaving this very lovable man. There would be no other love like Con. Heller knew that even if she married, there could be nothing like this night she'd shared with him. The memory would live like a fire in her mind, and she could take it out time after time in the cold years ahead and warm herself with it.

Easing away from him, she swung her legs over the edge of the bed. She would leave tonight. She couldn't imagine facing Con in the daytime. All she wanted to do was stay with him . . . and that couldn't be.

Downstairs she scrambled into her wrinkled clothes and tucked her purse under her arm. She paused to scribble two words on a pad of Andre Manhattan Hotel stationery, then hurried to the elevator. After one last look she left.

She used the employees' entrance, not wanting anyone to see her leaving the hotel so late. She had surprising luck in catching a cab. All during the ride to the warehouse, her thoughts were filled with Con. It was only when she opened her purse to pay the driver that she noticed the envelope stuffed inside. It was the one Con had received earlier.

She hurried inside the warehouse and took the massive elevator to the second floor, where her apartment was. She spent a minute greeting her exuberant dog, Hector, then opened the envelope. Ten one thousand dollar bills were inside.

For a moment shock muted her thoughts and emotions. How could he have known, she asked herself silently as she counted the money again. Then as the shock began to wear off, rage poured through her.

"I never *pay*," he'd said, but then, what was this for? Humiliation and fury started tears in her eyes, and she threw the money across the room.

"Damn him!" she screamed.

How could he have *paid* for what they had shared? He had told her he loved her, and then he had paid her as if she were no more than a very expensive hooker. How could he have lied like that?

She threw her arms around Hector as the tears poured down her face. "I hate him! I'll use his damned money, but I'll never stop hating him!"

Two

Con had been in a fury for weeks. Not one detective he'd sent out to trace Heller had come up with anything. All blind alleys! Where in hell had she gone?

"Dammit, Con, pay attention when I talk to you."

"What? Oh, sorry. I was thinking of something else."

"And so you've been doing for the last month, it seems. In love, boy?"

"No."

"Your mother says you're coming down with the flu. I think you've probably run afoul of one of those ladybirds you squire around. Am I right?"

"No."

Colonel Simon Wendel sighed, recognizing that implacable tone of his firstborn child. "You don't always have your own way with women, son. Look at me."

"You should know. Mother trolls you around like a hooked fish and you love it."

"Yes, your mother has a fatal attraction." Simon smiled with pleasure. "Just bought her a new dress. Charine designed it for her. Like her to look good."

Con smiled. "You know, Mother gives away enough discards to the Salvation Army to clothe the Bronx."

"Never be shabby with the ladies. It doesn't pay."

"It isn't that!" Con roared.

His father raised his brows. "I see."

Con paced his office. Where was she? There was still no sign, no trace of Heller. Had she stepped off the earth? He touched the spot; the mark had faded and gone now, where Heller had inadvertently scratched his neck when they had been in the throes of passion. That night had been fantastic, but no fantasy.

When he'd woken the next morning and there'd been no one next to him, he hadn't been worried, thinking that Heller was in the bathroom. It wasn't until he'd gone looking for her, roaming naked through the two-story suite, that he'd realized he was alone.

Bereft, he'd shouted her name over and over again. "Heller! Heller! Dammit, you can't leave me. Heller!"

She had taken the money. Why had she needed it? Why hadn't she confided in him? Her note said "Good-bye, Con," nothing more.

He pressed the intercom button on his phone. "John? Has Tabor called with any news?"

"Nothing, sir. Shall I try him again?"

"No." Con heard the sympathy in the other man's voice and ground his teeth. John, his personal assistant, had been with him a long time and knew his moods well. Often, especially when Con was feeling tense about business, he and John would have drinks or even dinner together. Today, though, like every other day since Heller had dropped out of his life, Con wanted no one's company but his own.

Heller Blane liked Barbados. She'd been there exactly one month. Her mother had died one month before she arrived. With a little less than a thousand dollars left from the money she'd gotten from Con, she had started over, changing her life completely.

When she'd gone to the Andre Manhattan Hotel to pick up, belatedly, her last paycheck, she'd seen a notice on the employees' bulletin board. They were hiring at the Andre Barbados. A recreation director with swimming, scuba, and boating skills was needed. She'd torn off the notice and stuffed it into her pocket. It was a far cry from the dream she'd had of being an actress on Broadway, her name in lights . . .

Later that same day she'd phoned the hotel in Barbados, described her qualifications, and said she could fly down the next day for an interview. She'd gotten the job.

Barbados was beautiful! The brochures did not do it justice. Sitting at her table near the beach, Heller breathed in the warm breeze and wondered if ever such sweet air could be imagined by man.

Already she felt at home on the island. If at times she was overcome by bittersweet memories of her mother, at least she knew her mother's last days had been as comfortable as she could make them. She did not deal as easily with her memories of Con. He was never far from her mind, and the thought of him filled her with throbbing emptiness.

There were crazy moments when she wished that

she and Con hadn't taken precautions, that they had conceived a child. Then she would realize how insane the idea was, and would force the thoughts of the wonderful passion that had been between them from her mind.

"Pardon me, Miss Blane." Heller looked up and saw a woman with two children standing in front of her table. "My name is Linda Jenkins and I've reserved the Hobie Cat for this hour. My children are going to use it while my husband and I go deep-sea fishing."

Heller glanced at her clipboard. "Jen and Tim Jenkins. I have the names right here, but . . ." She studied the two children and her smile slid off her face. "Surely you don't expect them to take the Cat out alone, Mrs. Jenkins. They're too young."

"They're very mature for their ages, Miss Blane," Mrs. Jenkins said huffily. "Timmy is large for a twelve-year-old and Jen is a very careful ten-year-old."

"I'm sorry, Mrs. Jenkins, I cannot let them take the Cat out on the sea alone."

"But—but my husband and I are going deep-sea fishing and the sea is so calm."

"Mrs. Jenkins, Barbados is the easternmost of all the Windward Islands. On this side the sea is usually calm, but that is a dangerous body of water for an expert, let alone a child. I cannot allow it."

"But we're guests here. We have rights." Mrs. Jenkins's rather weak chin wobbled. "I've never been deep-sea fishing."

Heller sighed, seeing the resigned, forlorn looks on the children's faces. "I have to stay here at my post, Mrs. Jenkins, and all the other attendants are busy, but I will try to take them out myself if I have time. For now they can remain on the beach with me and you can go deep-sea fishing."

"Oh, thank you. That will work out just fine." Mrs. Jenkins blew a kiss to her children, then sped away.

"You don't have to take us," Timmy said.

"But I will. Here, put this sunblock on all over your body. This is the tropics, and that sun is hot."

"You're really going to take us?" Jen asked.

"I am indeed." Heller smiled when both children beamed at her.

She wasn't able to arrange for anyone to watch her station during the morning, and decided to take the children out during her lunch break.

"Come on, you two, we're going sailing." The sun, at its zenith, was hot copper in the stinging blue sky when she pushed the twin-hulled Hobie Cat from the beach to the water.

"Get on right here, onshore. That's dangerous coral out there. Here we go." At once the sea breeze caught the tall sails, the Cat heeling just a bit before Heller corrected. It was going to be a very safe sail. She was taking no chances with these children.

The sea was a rolling azure mirror that reflected the hot sun at them, but a cooling breeze soothed them as they whisked past the beaches of the tropical island.

Once back onshore, the children tagged along with her, sitting at her table with her, or following her down the beach when she had to bring snorkeling equipment to a guest or arrange for someone to go waterskiing.

At the end of the day the mother gathered her children with no apology for being so long. "I hope they weren't any trouble."

"None at all," Heller said truthfully, smiling at the children. "We're going sailing tomorrow too." She grinned when the children whooped and Mrs. Jenkins looked disconcerted. "With your permission, of course."

"Of . . . of course."

After she was done for the day, Heller returned to her apartment, which was actually a small bungalow behind the hotel. The tiring day took its toll and she slept, not waking until after dark.

She showered and ate a light meal, then went for her evening stroll. Dressed in a strapless cotton sarong and leather sandals, she walked along the beach, watching the moon rise.

When she smelled smoke, she thought it was from a fire on the beach, then heard people screaming, "Fire!"

Turning, mouth agape, she could see smoke belching from the third floor of the hotel. Paralyzed, she stared at the tongues of flame for a moment before she began running back toward the hotel. As she neared it, she saw a small figure rush out onto the terrace of the third floor suite and call frantically for help.

Terror clamped Heller's throat shut as she recognized the person. It was Jen! She sprinted across the last few yards of sand to the back of the building and raced up the outside stairs. Choking as black smoke billowed around her, she struggled with the door to the suite. "Jen! Timmy! Answer me!"

"We can't get out! The fire's in the way!"

She threw herself against the strong wooden door, but to no avail. Then she spied a fire hose and hatchet in their glass case.

Bracing herself against the opposite wall, she thrust with both feet and broke the glass, setting off the alarm. It could barely be heard above the din of shouts and screams as people scrambled to safety.

Swinging the ax with all her might at the lock, Heller at last smashed it and thrust the door open. Smoke poured out, enveloping her. "Where are you?" she called. Tears flooded her eyes as she coughed repeatedly.

There was no answer. She would have to try to find them by crawling on the floor. Precious minutes sped by as she searched for the two children room by room, belly to the carpet. When she finally reached them, they were unconscious.

Knowing she couldn't go back the way she'd come, she dragged the children to the terrace. Flinging them down wasn't a great alternative, but it was her only choice. How could she climb down with them?

As she crawled out onto the terrace, she could hear people shouting.

She scrambled to the railing. "Here! We're here! Help me! Catch them, catch them!" She could barely get enough air in her parched lungs to speak. "Is someone down there? I have children."

"Yes, we have a blanket. We'll catch them. Hurry."

Heller felt the world spin around her as she thrust first one child, then the other over the railing. The thick smoke made it impossible to see which was which.

She had climbed over the railing herself and was about to go over, praying the blanket would hold her, when the world dropped away beneath her and she fell into oblivion.

Heller was in the hospital for four months. When the terrace had collapsed beneath her, she had plummeted the three stories, her fall only partially broken by a frangipani tree. Although the doctors told her

her injuries could have been much worse, she had still suffered a broken leg, a compound fracture of one shoulder, a severe concussion, and, of course, smoke inhalation and burns. Despite the painful injuries, she had been relieved to hear that Jen and Timmy had survived and would be all right.

She had been immobile for quite some time, then gradually had begun to move around, first with the aid of the nurses, and then on her own. At times the pain had been unbearable, but she had forced herself to keep going and to not favor her undamaged limbs. At last she had been released from the hospital, but she had had to go back three times a week for therapy.

She did not return to the Andre Barbados Hotel, to the little bungalow she had lived in before. She was a heroine and was to be treated as such. So she was moved to one of the expensive luxury villas of the Half Moon Cove Resort. The Half Moon, she was told, was owned by the Wendel Corporation, which also owned the Andre. She was even provided with a new wardrobe, for she'd lost a great deal of weight in the hospital and had dropped two sizes.

Another two months passed before the doctors declared her fit. Although she no longer needed physical therapy, they told her she must exercise regularly to regain her strength and stamina. But, they warned her, she must not overdo it.

Con smiled as he read the latest report from Barbados about Heller. No more physical therapy. She was at last fully recovered from her ordeal. Thank God. He'd been waiting forever for her to be well.

"It's a good report, isn't it?"

"What? Oh, yes, John, it is. What a time she's had."

"Will you be going down there?"

"Yes. Today."

John smiled. "Habersteen will expect you to inspect the renovations."

"Very amusing, John. I haven't waited all this time to see renovations."

"Shall I book the flight?"

"Right away. And thanks for the report." Con smiled at his assistant. He was sure John had thought he was crazy six months before when he'd discovered that one of the victims of the fire at the Barbados hotel had been a woman named Heller Blane. The coincidence of the unusual first name and the woman working for another Wendel hotel had convinced Con it was *his* Heller. He'd asked to have a picture made of the victim. The photograph of her, wan and thin, lying in a hospital bed, had merely confirmed what he knew. His first inclination had been to go there at once, but then he'd remembered how they'd parted. She might hate him now because of the money he'd put into her purse, thinking he'd been paying her for sleeping with him. Would his presence upset her so much that it would be detrimental to her recovery? With that in mind he'd remained in Chicago, receiving written reports twice a day on her condition, and phone calls when her condition was critical. More than once he'd packed a bag, only to unpack it when she'd recovered from a setback. The medical staff and insurance investigators who reported to him daily were completely convinced that Heller was his cousin.

Often he'd had difficulty concentrating on work, too tense to think of anything but seeing Heller again. He'd never gotten the night they'd spent together out of his mind. Visions of the two of them writhing on his bed, captured by the most passionate physical love he'd ever know, had left him sleepless for months.

Now, at last, he'd be with her again.

"Since you're fully recovered, Miss Blane, I thought you would be pleased to meet with the head of the corporation."

"That's very nice, and please don't think I'm ungrateful, Mr. Habersteen." Heller looked around her opulent suite. Even after two months she still wasn't used to living there. "I really don't think it's necessary for me to see Mr. Wendel."

"But you must. He'll be here today." Mr. Habersteen, the manager of the Half Moon and the Andre, glanced anxiously at his watch. "I'm sure he's been picked up by now, so I should get back to my office to greet him. We'll be joining you sometime in the evening, I'm sure. Mr. Wendel will want to go over the books and look at the renovations first."

"Of course." Heller stared at the door after Mr. Habersteen had bustled away. Mr. Wendel must be a crusty curmudgeon to get his staff in such a tizzy.

Feeling restless, she wandered around the suite. This was her first day without physical therapy, and already she felt sedentary. She ran up the stairs to her bedroom and fumbled through the dresser drawers until she found a new swimsuit. For her therapy, she had swum in the hospital pool every day. Pools bored her, though, and she longed for a swim in the sea.

She quickly pulled on the orange suit, then gaped

at her reflection. The suit fit like a second skin, and was cut indecently high, almost to the waist, at the outer thighs. "Goodness. I look like an orange nude." Talking to herself had become a habit during her long hospitalization.

She grabbed a towel, then paused to stare at her reflection again. There were a few burn scars on her arms and legs, but they were barely noticeable and she ignored them. Instead, she gazed at her face, now pronouncedly heart-shaped with prominent cheekbones. Gone were her full breasts and hips. She was svelte, though not completely lacking in curves. She looked wraithlike, but she felt almost as strong as she had been before the fire.

What would Con think of her if he could see her now? Would he like this new body, or would he prefer the old one? Dreamily, she imagined the expression on his face when he saw her, his astonishment, then his pleasure. He would smile that warm, wonderful smile of his, reach out his arms to her, pull her close, and—

No! Ruthlessly, she pushed the daydream away. She fully accepted that Con would always be a part of her, but refused to dwell on what could have been. Probably no man would ever get as close to her as he had, and she'd have to learn to live with that.

Pushing thoughts of Con into a cubbyhole in the back of her mind, she left her suite and jogged slowly across the wide swath of sand to the water. She noticed the tightness in her shoulder and leg but ignored it. Soon even that would be gone. There was no dangerous coral in the water at the front of her suite, just firm sand and clear sea.

Plunging into the sea made her catch her breath, but the revivifying rolling saltwater had her gasping with pleasure after the first few seconds. Striking out strongly, she gloried in a sense of well-being and pride at having recovered so well from her injuries.

When she felt the first twinges of fatigue, she stopped, treading water as she turned back to the shore. She was startled to see how far she had come. She hoped she wouldn't have any trouble getting back.

Pacing herself and swimming with careful control, she kept her gaze fixed on her white villa. When she finally reached the beach, she was reeling with fatigue. She had to pause to take several deep, shuddering breaths. She'd swum too far.

Scooping up her towel, she trudged slowly across the hot sand, feeling the Barbadian sun beat down on her bent head. A long, cool drink and bed. That's what she needed. The head of the hotel chain wouldn't be seeing her until the evening, so she had time. Mr. Habersteen had intimated the executive would want to see the renovations that had been going on almost since the day after the fire.

She tiredly pushed open the door to her villa and stepped into its coolness. The sudden darkness after the brilliant sun made her pause on the threshold.

Con stared at her framed in the doorway, the sunlight outlining every line and curve of her. It was like the dream he had most nights. She was standing in front of him, gazing his way, though he was aware she hadn't seen him yet.

She was unbelievably slender. Her full hips had narrowed, and her breasts, though still nicely rounded, were smaller. Even her fabulous long legs were slimmer. He knew he could circle his thumb and forefinger around her ankle. If anything, she was sexier than ever, more beautiful, fragile, yet so very tough.

His insides knotted painfully at the thought of her being in that fire, of falling three stories and breaking her leg and shoulder. She could have died. Involuntarily he reached for her.

Seeing a movement in the dim room, Heller pulled her towel protectively around her. "Who is it?"

"You should have stayed, Heller. I might well have paid for another night." Con moved into the slatted sunlight coming through the wooden blinds.

"Con!" Heller took a step backward, as though she would flee.

"No. Stay. Don't run."

"I can't run," she said faintly as her rubbery knees gave way.

He caught her before she hit the floor. "Dammit, what have you been doing?"

"Swimming. What else?" She fainted.

Lifting her high into his arms, Con stared at her pallid face. Her delicate bones seemed to poke through her parchmentlike skin. "Oh, no, you don't, Heller," he murmured. "You're not leaving me again. I have you now, and I'm keeping you."

Three

After carefully laying Heller on the couch, Con called the front desk. "This is Conrad Wendel. I want a doctor sent to Miss Blane's villa at once." His sharp tone brooked no argument.

He carried her upstairs to her bedroom, stripped off her wet suit, and covered her with the bedspread. Back down in the kitchen he wrapped some ice in a towel, then returned to her and placed the ice on her warm forehead.

Jagged lightning cut across the sky and thunder rumbled in its wake as a tropical storm hit full force. Still Heller did not stir, and Con watched her worriedly as he rose to close the blinds.

She started to come around just as there was a knock on the door downstairs. Con ran from the room to let the doctor in, then sprinted back up the stairs, the doctor at his heels.

When he burst into the room, Heller opened her eyes. "Oh, no," she breathed. "Not you."

"Yes, me." He could see the doctor was surprised at his clipped, angry tone, but didn't care. "Would you examine the patient, please? She fainted. I'll be just outside."

Con paced the narrow hall that connected the two bedrooms and bath on the second floor. Damn the staff! Why had they given her a two-story villa when she could have had his one-story place?

The waning storm mirrored his agitation.

It seemed hours before the doctor appeared in the hallway, shutting the door behind him.

"Well? Is she all right?"

"As well as anyone can be after undergoing the multiple traumas that she's had. Fatigue is the big thing right now. She tells me that she probably swam too far and—"

"What? Dammit, why wasn't anyone with her? Where are her nurses?"

"Miss Blane has never wanted nursing care, Mr. Wendel, and she seems well enough to care for herself—"

"Well, she isn't. She needs care and she'd going to have it. Thank you for coming, Doctor. Good-bye."

Con waited until the doctor had left the villa, then opened the bedroom door. Heller stared defiantly at him. "You've been traumatized with broken bones, shock, and weight loss. How dare you endanger your life by swimming too far out into the sea?"

She turned her head. "There is a money debt between us, which I intend to repay. I'm not a prostitute. I had already begun a special savings account before . . ." She swallowed. "If I'd known that you were the C. Wendel who initials the toilet paper in this establishment, I would have left a long time ago."

"I know that. And I do not initial the toilet paper, though I do keep a weather eye on things."

"A weather eye? Is that what you call it? Lord, when the staff knew you were coming, they went into an absolute snit. Every one of them has been out of breath since you called."

"I won't let you leave me again, Heller."

"There is only a financial debt between us," she said tightly, her teeth clenched.

"We'll be moving into my villa today. It's roomier and you'll have more privacy. Your nurses will be able to stay overnight if need be."

"Forget it! I don't need nursing and I won't have it."

"Fine, then I'll nurse you."

"No!"

"Yes. When you're well enough, we'll be going back to New York."

"No, my job is here and I support myself. Get yourself a global mobile from that diamond set of yours and forget me. I don't play in your league."

"Thank you for putting me in my place, Heller, but I had better tell you that I don't take orders well. Though you may try to direct my life, and succeed, you will not take yourself out of it. Save yourself some effort and don't try."

She lifted her head, pointed her small, firm chin. "Don't try to dictate to me, buster. It won't work."

"Darling, I wouldn't dream of it. You will be doing the directing, not me. Just don't try getting away from me."

She stared silently at him for a minute. "I want to get up. Leave the room."

"All right, if that's what you want. But I have seen you in the buff. I was the one who undressed you before the doctor came, and that night in the Andre Manhattan Hotel . . ."

"Leave, monster."

Heller stayed under the covers even after Con had left, his throaty chuckle coiling around the room like a silken lasso.

Damn, damn, damn the man! It had taken so many sleepless nights and long, arduous days for her to come to terms with living without Con. Now he was implying that he could breeze back into her life, shattering her fragile barriers.

She sat up and swung her feet to the floor, then remained motionless until a wave of dizziness passed. In the bathroom she showered, letting the cool water sluice over her heated body. As she soaped and shampooed to remove the salt from her skin, she lectured herself about Con.

She would not let him into her life. Anger that she had needed his money, had used it, and now had to repay surged through her. She was not a prostitute. He would get his money back. She was healthy, and her bones had knitted well. She could go back to New York and try the theater as she'd always wanted to do, put the past behind her.

She donned a fine cotton sarong in hues of peach and turquoise, then applied apricot foundation and lip gloss. After taking several deep breaths, she opened the door and marched downstairs.

Con immediately rose from the couch and walked toward her, holding out his hands to her.

His twisted smile when she avoided his touch passed over her like a feathery caress. "Don't fight it," he said. "You're the same woman who made beautiful love to me eight months ago. There should be no shyness between us."

"I'm not shy," she shot back at him. He was a rat for mentioning that night, she mused.

"You're very slender but still gorgeous. Your eyes have taken on an almond shape, lending you an air of mystery." His gaze touched every inch of her. "In fact, your face has an Oriental cast now. Dynamite with your coloring." He reached out and touched her short, curling golden hair. "I miss your hair. Why did you cut it?"

"They had to shave my head because I'd gashed the back of it and needed stitches."

Con swallowed painfully, imagining an unconscious Heller, her body swaddled in bandages, suspended in traction, an attendant shaving her head. "Damn that fire!"

He pulled her close and brought his mouth to hers, worrying her soft lips until they parted for him. His tongue touched hers over and over again in a long, soul-stretching kiss. With their lips still touching, he spoke to her. "I could have lost you, Heller. It took me too long to find you. That has been my personal hell these last months. If I had ever suspected you would be trapped in a fire, I would have moved heaven and earth to get to you."

Heller had pulled away to speak, when there was a knock on the door.

"I'll be right there." Con called out. His rough reply was accompanied by a scowl. Convulsively, he tightened his hold on Heller. "We'll have to answer that."

"I hope you're not going to yell at whoever it is," she said, freeing herself and moving away from him.

"I'd like to maim anyone who interrupts us." He

caught her hand, entwining her fingers with his as he opened the door. "You're here to move Miss Blane's things?" he asked the two men in hotel uniforms.

"Yes sir, we are."

"This is a lovely villa," Heller said faintly.

"Yes, but you need all the amenities, darling. We'll have our own pool besides the sea, and we'll have privacy."

"Is that the royal 'we'?"

"Do I hear a touch of acid in your voice?"

"More than a touch." She was angry at the easy way Con was moving in on her life. "*I* say what I do, and I haven't given anyone else the right to do that in my life." She glared at him. "Ten thousand dollars gives you no rights over me."

"Understood. Indulge me on this and then we'll do it your way."

"Balderdash!" She wanted to tell him to parasail out to sea, but with the two men waiting patiently for instructions and Con's hot eyes on her, her resolve wavered. She nodded her head once, sharply.

In less than half an hour her belongings were packed up and put on the golf-cart-type vehicle that the hotel used.

When Heller saw a similar vehicle behind it, she said to Con, "I can walk."

"You've had ample exercise today with your swim."

"I am amazed that *you* can walk upright," she said caustically. "It must be such a temptation for acquaintances to drop-kick you."

He helped her into the passenger seat and kissed her ear. "Please don't do that. It might interfere with our life . . . temporarily."

"Permanently, maybe."

"Never. Nothing is coming between us, Heller." He

started the vehicle and wheeled it down the wide, curving path.

"Aren't you afraid you'll take out a few guests at this speed?" she asked, hanging on to the side of the cart.

"Why did you need ten thousand dollars so desperately, Heller?" Con turned onto a narrower path marked Private, weaving among the sumptuous flora indigenous to Barbados. Stopping in front of a white villa three times the size of the one she'd just left, he turned to look at her. Her terse note—"Good-bye, Con"—was an acid in his soul yet.

"Gambling debts?" he asked.

She shook her head.

"Tell me."

Heller released a shuddering sigh. What was wrong with telling him about her mother now? Everyone who had anything to do with that time in her life was gone. Weren't they? "Medical care for someone I cared for deeply and who was too proud to ask for help of any sort. That's all I'm going to say. It was too little too late."

"I'm sorry." He caressed a silky golden curl, smiling at her while his insides roiled with jealousy. "Was it a lover? A friend?"

"My mother. And I won't play Twenty Questions about my life, Con."

"You should have come to me and not run. I would have provided the best care your mother could have had."

"She had the best." She stepped from the cart and walked toward the villa. After a moment, Con followed her.

As she entered the villa, made of quarried coral, Heller instantly felt cooler. "Air-conditioning?"

"Yes, but the Roman kind. Cooled water is run through pipes in the ceiling and floor, keeping the house very comfortable. There's a solar collector that can heat the water as well as the house, but it's rarely used."

She gazed around the massive living room. "It's very spacious."

"Yes," he answered, chuckling. "Shall I give you the real estate rundown? This is a four-bedroom suite. Two bedrooms are in the master section and two are on the guest side of the house. There is a library, kitchen, dining room, and this is the living room. Plus, of course, there is a lanai and terrace that look out on the sea. Like it?"

"Very much, but, Con—"

"No buts, darling. We're staying here." He approached her. "Have I told you that you have an Oriental look to you now?"

"You mentioned it."

"You were sexy enough before. Now you're devastating." He watched her blood flow and ebb in her face. "Why should that embarrass you, love? We've been very close."

"Your smile is satanic, did you know that?"

"I've been called a devil a time or two."

"Type casting." She took a step back from him as a fire blazed in his emerald eyes. It wasn't fury she saw there, but unquenchable desire. "Con, the only thing between us is the money I owe you."

"I think there's more."

She swallowed hard. Visions of how they'd been together blossomed in her head. "No! I won't be your mistress." Once more she stepped back.

"Then be my wife."

"Ridiculous!"

"When did you develop that squeak in your voice?"

"Don't fool yourself into thinking I'm mouselike."

"Never, my sensuous termagant, would I think that."

"Good. I'm going for a walk."

"Let me put your sun prevention on you first. You know your skin is still sensitive from the burns and you're not supposed to get one bit of sun on it. I've talked to the doctors and—"

"Steamrolled them, you mean." She dropped her voice to bass level. "This is Captain Bligh speaking."

"Darling, I was very gentle with all your doctors."

His grin drove her mad. "Yes, I can imagine." Her voice dropped several decibels again. "Doctor, if your answer isn't right, I'll waltz you sweetly to the guillotine."

"Something like that," he admitted, unfazed by her assessment. He was so damned glad to see her alive and well, he didn't care what she said or did as long as they weren't separated. It hadn't been until he'd seen her again that he'd realized he'd been figuratively holding his breath, not believing she was real until he touched her. The familiar ache that had been inside him since that night in New York was at last fading.

"I'll rub your body with the proper lotion, then we'll go for a short walk."

Enraged by his assumption of command, she said perversely, "I'd like to swim instead."

"Not after what happened this morning."

"All right. Then I'll just go for a longer swim tomorrow."

There was a roaring in his ears, and he felt as though his body had turned to fire and ice simultaneously. "Don't . . . you . . . ever . . . put . . . your-self . . . at risk like that again."

She was stunned by the intensity of his reaction, and held out her hand to him. He was ashen. "I didn't mean it, Con."

"I hope not. Now, promise me you won't do anything so foolhardy again."

"I like to swim."

"Fine. Just use some common sense. Not too much strenuous swimming since you've been so ill."

"Con—"

"Do you have any lotion, or should I phone for some?"

She drew back at his harsh tone. "I have some that the doctor gave me." She turned away and started down a hall to what she thought was her bedroom.

"No, darling." He took her hand and led her the other way. "That's where I'm sleeping. You're in the master suite. The view is better and there's more room."

"I don't need—"

"Where's the lotion?"

"Why are you in such a temper?"

"Because I can't get the vision of you in a fire out of my mind!"

Silence surrounded them as she stared at him. "It was awful," she whispered at last. "I was so afraid."

"But you went up those stairs and got those two children . . . through the smoke . . . and flames." His voice was hoarse, his eyes glittering. "Then that damned balcony collapsed underneath you."

"I had to do it."

He pulled her into his arms. "And I have to keep you safe. No, don't say any more. Let me hold you."

She leaned against him and at once the hot memories of being together in the Andre Manhattan erupted in her mind.

"You're remembering the Andre, aren't you, Heller?" he asked. His face was pressed against her hair, and he inhaled the still-familiar fragrance of her body.

"Stop trying to be a mind reader," she said. "You don't have the credentials."

"Darling, how you talk. When you get angry, your breasts push against me in a lovely way."

"Lecher!" Heller tried to push back from him, but she was held fast. "You wanted me to get the lotion for my skin."

"Ploy, darling, but I'll let you go this time." When she turned away, he let his hand feather over her backside. "You still have the most beautiful body in the world, and I'm going to see to it that you get back to full health."

She quivered in response. "I'm almost there now," she said without turning, then hastened into the spacious bedroom. She shut the door behind her and leaned against it, closing her eyes. No one should exude such electricity, she thought. Con could flatten Barbados with the charges that flew off him.

She opened her eyes and looked around the unfamiliar room, the walked over to the built-in wall of drawers. In the top drawer she found her favorite suit, a one-piece in bright turquoise. After changing, she flung a terry-cloth jacket over her shoulders, grabbed the tall bottle of lotion on the dresser, and left the room.

Con was in the hallway waiting for her, dressed in

a brief black bathing suit. His appreciative gaze ran over her. "You were too long."

"A minute." ·

"That's too long." He leaned down and kissed her nose. "You have great legs."

"How ever do you keep your mind on business when you're so preoccupied with—"

"With you? With making love to you? Touching you all over with my mouth, letting . . ." He kissed the fingers she pressed against his lips. "You asked."

"I'll remember not to call you on anything. Did you inherit your wealth? Do you not have to work, and that's why you're so concentrated on other things?" She watched the blood run up his face, his mouth tighten. "That was crass and I've insulted you," she said quietly. "I shouldn't have said—"

"No!" The word was fired from his mouth. "For the record, I did come into money from my grand-parents. My parents, who are wealthy in their own right, carried on the tradition of the hotels started by my mother's father. My father's parents were in steel and offshore drilling. With my money I—"

"Please, don't tell me any more." Heller shifted from one foot to the other. "My remarks were un-called for and I apologize."

"Accepted. But you still should know that I began Wendel Communications on my own. We now own five television stations and twice that many radio stations. WC produces shows for television and we are currently purchasing a movie studio with affili-ates in London and the Far East—"

"Con, stop."

He inclined his head. "You should know your hus-band's worth, since it will be yours one day."

"Will not." Heller was out of breath, off balance. "I'm going for that walk."

"First the lotion."

"I can do it."

"Don't be ridiculous. Come out on the terrace and I'll do it in the shade of the trees."

Heller followed him because she had the feeling there would be a brouhaha if she balked. Once under the latticework shade of the gently swaying trees, she stood still so he could apply the lotion.

It took every bit of strength that she had not to collapse in a heap when Con began at her bare feet, smoothing the emollient slowly and thoroughly into her skin. In slow stages he moved upward. His touch on her inner thigh was her undoing, and she stepped back.

"What is it, Heller? Did I touch a tender spot?"

"You could say that." She coughed to clear the squeak from her voice. Her blood began to race at the hot look in his eyes. "I can finish the rest."

"Not really. Turn around and I'll do your back."

She gritted her teeth and closed her eyes as his strong hands moved over her spine, his long fingers probing under her arms and at the high cut of her suit.

"There, that should protect you."

She wanted to laugh. Protected! She was strewn every which way along the terrace. He had torn her apart!

"I really don't think you should go for a walk, Heller. You've had your exercise for the day. Why don't we just sit here and have a cool drink and watch the sea?"

"But—"

"Admit you're ready to stretch out and relax."

She hesitated, then nodded.

"I'll order some drinks for us."

When he returned, she was stretched out on a lounger. He lay down next to her, and she turned her head to face him. "Con, I have the feeling you've known I was here for some time. Have you?"

Just then the buzzer at the villa door sounded and Con rose to answer it. He came back with a tray of sunbursts, a cooling drink of seltzer water, orange juice, and sliced limes. He handed one to her and reseated himself.

"Well?" she asked.

He swirled the ice around in his glass. "I've known since the fire that you were here. It seemed wise to let you get your strength back before coming to see you." His eyes met hers challengingly. Before she could reply, though, he leaned over and pressed his mouth to the sensitive skin where her hip and thigh met.

"Conrad!"

He heard the lacing of panic in her voice. "Don't be afraid of me, darling. I'll never hurt you."

"Too late," she muttered.

"Tell me when I've hurt you."

"Con, let go of this—"

"Never!"

"You don't know me, I don't know you."

"Ask me anything."

"I—I have nothing to ask." Heller felt storm-tossed and out of control.

"If you think of anything, ask." Con let one finger trail up her bare arm. "By the way, I thought you'd like to dine at The Plantation this evening. Sound good?'

"Sure. But it will cost the earth."

He chuckled. "Are you going to keep a close watch on my bank account when we're married, darling?"

"Con, please don't talk that way." He could never know that she might not be safe until she died. Even though things have been quiet for almost two years, she couldn't be sure that the Domini brothers wouldn't find her. The thought of involving Con with them made her want to retch.

Anger flashed across his face like summer lightning. "Stop putting up barriers. Heller."

"I don't have to put them up." She pushed his hand away. "They're already there."

"Name one," he demanded roughly.

"Good relationships don't start on the basis of sex and money or a combination of such."

"Bull! It wasn't like that and you know it."

Heller blinked at his furious expression. "My family is . . . was middle class and—"

"Tell me about your family."

"It's not relevant."

"I think it is. Since we will be living together in New York, I think everything about you is relevant."

She thought it best to ignore his comment about living together. "My parents are dead. My father played cello in a symphony orchestra, my mother was an accountant. When my father was killed in a plane accident on his way back from a performance, she started a small accounting business at home. She died earlier this year."

"The money was for her care."

"Yes."

The unspoken told him as much as the spoken. For a short time there was silence between them.

Heller cleared her throat. "When I return to New

York, I'll be sharing a place with a friend who has a warehouse in the West Village."

"I see."

Con felt a burning desire for the sensuous, confident woman beside him, but he had an urge to throttle her too. Sophisticated firebrand was the description that fit her. Was that a contradiction in terms? Whatever she was and whatever she was hiding, she would not get away from him again. Somehow he would discover what had frightened her and handle that too. She was an itch he couldn't scratch. "I searched for you for a long time. Maybe if I'd found you sooner—"

"Those children might have died."

He lifted her hand and kissed it. "True."

Heller couldn't help smiling at him. It was so wonderful being with Con. She should savor this time. Seize the moment! Still, he expected too much from her, expected a future. Couldn't he see how different they were? She would never fit into his world. It would be so easy just to let him take care of her, him, with all his money, but her pride wouldn't stand for it. And she'd pay him back his ten thousand dollars if it killed her!

She turned a level gaze on him. "Nothing's changed, Con. We met, we separated. That's all."

"No, Heller," he said silkily. "It's barely begun."

He was sparring with her, not conversing. Words were epees with which to slice and feint. Each was searching for the opening to deliver the coup de grâce. Though traces of her ordeal still showed in her face, there was a fierce light of determination in her eyes. "You'll be able to tell me more about your mother and your accident when we're back in New

York." In bittersweet challenge he tossed the words at her like a gauntlet.

"There's one night between us and an IOU for ten thousand dollars, Con." He couldn't be included in her life. If the Domini brothers ever found her . . .

Conrad watched as myriad expressions chased themselves across her face. He was walking a tight-rope with Heller. She could bolt if he pushed too hard. At the same time, he was determined not to be thwarted. Jousting with her didn't lessen his want of her, or his need. "Why won't you tell me about your family?" he asked. She blinked, but otherwise did not show that she might be disconcerted by the change of subject.

"I told you they were dead. That's all there is."

"Shouldn't I be the judge of that?"

She shook her head.

"I know you quit your job at the Andre the day after the night we spent together. But you didn't come right to Barbados. According to your person-nel file, you'd been here only a short time before the fire."

"I did a little wandering."

"On ten thousand dollars you could do that."

"What? Oh, yes, the money. I didn't use it for that. For my mother . . . her debts."

"Is there any left?"

"Very little, but I will be getting a job soon."

"I see." He watched that small chin come up, saw again the determined glitter in her eyes, and knew he had a fight on his hands. "Perhaps you should rest now. We'll talk more later. After dinner I thought we might go dancing if you're not too tired. I recall you like to dance." He pushed himself up off the lounger and strode back into the house.

Heller remained where she was, trembling. The man was a bloody hurricane, she thought, flattening anything and everything in his path. He would destroy her, too, if she let him. He wrung her out emotionally, more than anything or anyone in her life. Perhaps if their beginning hadn't been so unorthodox . . . perhaps if there were no more Domini brothers . . .

He'd mentioned marriage, but that could never be.

She returned to her bedroom and lay on the bed, staring up at the cream-colored ceiling. "Mother, I wish you could be with me now, to talk about Con. I wish it hadn't taken death for me to be able to stop worrying about your safety." Closing her eyes, she tried not think that she, too, might still be a target of the men who'd tried to stop her mother.

When she wakened, Heller glanced at the clock. She was startled by the late hour and hurriedly showered. Con was taking her out to dinner. No matter how many times and ways she lectured herself to be sensible, she couldn't smother the bubble of anticipation that was rising in her.

When she opened her closet, she was taken aback. There were the usual cotton sarongs that belonged to her, but there was also a coral-hued silk one. Her hand gravitated to it and clutched it. She knew instinctively that Con had purchased it for her. The wisest thing to do would be to leave it hanging in the closet, but the temptation to wear the wonderful dress was too much.

After she was ready. She wondered where Con was. She walked down the center hall to the immense sitting room. Beyond it was the lanai, and she thought she saw movement out there. She started toward it, then stopped when Con stepped from the shadows. "You're a goddess, Heller. And I will never give you up."

Their dinner was a kaleidoscopic dream enfolding them both, the conversation was sporadic. There was little need for words. Dancing was one more bond between them.

When they returned to the villa, Heller was both disappointed and relieved that Con, after kissing her deeply several times, went to his own room. But still, all night long he was in her dreams.

Four

By the end of the next day Heller knew she had to leave Barbados. Although she couldn't think of a more wonderful place to convalesce, Con was driving her crazy. He'd brought her breakfast in bed that morning. He'd looked so sexy and appealing, she'd barely been able to swallow the luscious fruit and strong, flavorful coffee. After she'd showered and dressed, he had walked along the beach with her. She had been surprised by his casualness and his cheerful, even boyish, high spirits. Here in the beautiful tropical paradise Con completely lost that hard edge she'd been aware of in New York, and even yesterday, and became a genial, relaxing companion.

Later, after he'd spent several hours on the phone handling business problems, he'd swum laps with her in the villa's pool, matching her stroke for stroke. He'd helped her dry off, then once more smoothed lotion over her tingling body. She'd begun to melt under his caress, and only the memory of the money he'd paid her for sleeping with him saved her.

He'd taken her out to dinner again, and over a delicious seafood salad had finally explained to her how he'd known she needed ten thousand dollars.

"The bartender at the Andre told me," he said. "I didn't know why you needed ten thousand dollars, but I knew I wanted to help you. I put the money into your purse when you turned toward the window in the suite, but I assumed I'd have the chance to talk with you about it the next morning."

She looked away. "I know I shouldn't have left like that, but . . . I was confused."

"You don't need to be confused any longer." He took her hand in his. "We're together now, and we'll stay that way."

She'd had great trouble falling asleep that night.

Three days later Heller told Con she was ready to return to New York.

"I can't live off your company's largess any longer," she said. "I've already contacted a friend of mine who owns the apartment where I lived before. She has plenty of room for me there. And I'm sure I'd have a better chance getting a job in Manhattan than here."

Con didn't argue with her. He immediately called Mr. Habersteen to reserve two seats to New York on the next available fligh:. Maids arrived to pack their clothes. Heller barely had time for one last swim before they were on their way to the airport.

"I want you to stay with me," Con said as they

rode in a limousine from Kennedy Airport to Manhattan.

"But you live in Chicago."

"Not anymore. I'm in the process of relocating to New York." His significant look told her why. "Heller, I want to take care of you."

"I don't think that would be a good idea," she said. "I need to be independent for a while, Con. I need to stand on my own feet and figure out what I want to do with my life."

"I'll let you have independence. You can have your own room, your own car. You can come and go as you please—"

"No! I don't want all that. I want to deal with this my way."

"Deal with what? Tell me, Heller." He waited, but she was silent. "All right, I won't press you. You can be on your own, but I want to know where you are."

"Fair enough."

For the rest of the trip Heller was unaccountably depressed at the thought of being apart from Con. Not only was she unable to forget the night she'd spent with him at the Andre Manhattan, she had also fallen a little more in love with him these past few days.

When they arrived at her friend's warehouse, he helped her from the limo and kissed her twice, but let the chauffeur accompany her upstairs with her luggage.

By the next morning Heller was firmly ensconced in the warehouse apartment owned by her friend, Doodie Kleinfeltz. She had met Doodie almost two years before at an art exhibit, and they had quickly become good friends. Last year, when Doodie had gone off to Paris to study art, she had let Heller stay in her apartment rent-free. Now she was delighted to have Heller back.

"And you can stop talking about leaving, Heller. I won't let you. I know you got spoiled living here alone, but there's plenty of room. I sleep in that little room off my studio. We'll have to share the bath and that's no fun. And you still have to bang on the hot water heater to get it going. But we're going to have a great time."

"Thanks, Doodie." Heller hugged her friend. "And thanks for bringing Hector back." Heller scratched the dog behind the ears, laughing when he whined with pleasure. Before she had left New York, she had sent Hector to stay with Doodie's uncle, who owned a small farm in New Jersey. When Heller had told Doodie she was coming back to New York, Doodie had retrieved Hector.

"How's the commercial art field doing?" Heller asked.

"I feed myself and pay the monthly fees on this place. On the side I'm illustrating a children's book. If it does well, I could get others." She smiled and pushed her thick glasses back up on her nose. "As long as Leonard thinks I'm great, I'll make it."

Heller shook her head. "You and Leonard Billings. It's great. You've been friends since, what, third grade?"

"And I've been in love with him since the fourth grade." Doodie shrugged. "We're saving to get married. He's planning on coming to New York soon and moving in with me."

"When he does, I'll leave."

"No need. I told you, there's plenty of room."

"Thanks, Doodie."

Later that day, when Doodie was working and

Heller was perusing the want ads, Con called. "I'm doing fine," Heller told him. "I'm reading the want ads."

"Come to work at Wendel's."

"Thanks, but I think as long as I'm in New York, I'm going to contact an agent a friend of mine once had and see if he'll represent me."

"I didn't know you were interested in show business. Wait a minute. I think I know someone who might be able to help you."

"But . . ." The phone clicked in Heller's ear. That man steamrolled everything!

When the phone rang again, Heller was once more engrossed in the want ads.

"This is Manny Levin, Ms. Blane," said a man with a distinctive New York accent. "Mr. Wendel said that you were interested in auditions, right? There's not much going on right now, just auditions for a new musical, a couple of dramas. Some off-Broadway stuff. Get the picture? Competition's stiff for anything like this. Only a couple of parts to be cast. I'll give you the details and you can use my name. Got an Equity card? Good. Let me know how it goes. See ya."

Talking with Manny Levin, Heller thought, was like talking with a machine gun. Still, she was elated with the list he'd given her.

It wasn't easy to find an acting job in Manhattan, even with a list from Manny Levin, and the turndowns she received reinforced that.

No way was she going to accept Con's offer of a job with his corporation, though. Such proximity to him day after day would melt any resistance to him she could muster. Being with him for eight-hour stretches would be a sweet torture.

She'd been in town for nearly a week when the last audition Manny had told her about was held. It was a musical, and the line outside the theater was awesome. A true cattle call! Although she had worked on her audition pieces these past several days, Heller wasn't exactly brimming with hope as she stepped out on the stage. She had dressed appropriately in a leotard and tights, and hoped they'd give her a chance.

"You don't have much background," the director said. He was sitting with a few other men in the third row.

"Not a lot, but I can dance and sing," she said confidently.

The man sighed tiredly and shrugged. "Okay. Let's hear you sing, then you can dance."

She sang her mother's favorite song, "Danny Boy," and the memory of her beloved mother gave a poignancy to her voice. After that she did a dance number she remembered from "Forty-second Street," which she'd acted in a few summers before.

"Okay," the director said, breaking her off in mid-dance. "Wait over there, will you?"

Heller blinked in surprise and nodded.

Much to her shock, she got a small but fun part in the play.

Too bemused to believe her luck, she walked all the way downtown to the apartment, not even thinking of looking for a bus. A job in the theater! What luck! If she could only pull it off, her life might take just the turn it needed.

Now she needn't worry about taking a job from Con. The power he held over her already made her shiver. Every evening she saw him or at least talked to him, and every night she went to bed with her mind filled with his image, her body longing for his touch. But she mustn't grow dependent on him—or possibly put him in danger.

When she got home she called him to thank him. That night he brought over Chinese food to celebrate.

"Where's Doodie?" he asked as he pulled white cartons from the bags.

"She teaches class tonight," Heller said. She was unaccountably shy and nervous about being alone with him tonight.

He poured plum wine for both of them. "So tell me about this play. When does it open?"

"Very soon. Actually, it's already opened in Philadelphia and they needed to fill only a few parts today. I don't like to capitalize on anyone's bad luck, but it seems the woman who had *my* part fell and broke her leg. Since the part is mostly dancing, they had to recast it."

"What about *your* broken leg?"

"It's completely healed. And the dancing isn't very strenuous."

"Well, I look forward to seeing it. What's the play called?"

"*Under the Lights.*"

"I've heard of it. Tomorrow I'll order a block of tickets for opening night."

She gave him a curious look. "You may not like it."

"I'll take a chance. When are you on?"

"Right after the intermission."

He lifted his glass. "Let's drink to your success."

She clinked her glass against his. "To success."

After they finished eating they sat on the rug in the living room. For several minutes the only sound in the room was the gentle rhythms of Al Jarreau.

Heller could feel a tension building between them, a palpable sexual tension. They hadn't been alone together since they'd left Barbados.

When Con urged her to lie back on the rug and stretched out beside her, her breathing almost stopped. "Do you remember?" he whispered.

"Yes."

"There's that squeak in your voice again." He pressed his mouth to hers, gently easing her lips apart, his tongue touching hers.

In moments they were locked together, arms and legs entwined.

At last Heller pulled her mouth away. "Doodie . . . she'll be coming home soon." Breath rasped from her body. Her clenching hands released him reluctantly.

Con, his hair tousled, his eyes dark with passion, stared down at her. "You want me, Heller, and I sure as hell want you. Live with me."

"I can't."

"Dammit!" He rolled to his feet, his body aroused and tense. He glanced down at her once, then stalked from the apartment.

Heller was in bed but not asleep when Doodie returned at ten o'clock. Dry-eyed and hurting, she greeted the hazy dawn. She was as wide awake as she had been when she climbed into bed.

For a week she heard nothing from Con. The rehearsals were a blessing, allowing her to punish her body until fatigue claimed her at night.

One afternoon Heller got out of rehearsal early. Feeling the need for some fresh air, she decided against taking the bus and began walking south toward Greenwich Village. As always when her mind was unoccupied, her thoughts turned to Con. She told herself she should be glad he was staying away from her, giving her the space she needed, but in truth she missed him. She was debating calling him as soon as she got home, when she heard a shout. Looking up, she saw she had inadvertently walked too far west, and had strayed into one of the worst sections of Manhattan.

She was about to head east down a cross street, when she became aware of a commotion on the far side of the avenue. A small young boy was in the center of a circle of older bigger boys, his expression tight and determined as he faced very poor odds.

When one of the older boys struck him, knocking him down, Heller sprinted across the avenue, ignoring the irate honking.

"Get off him!" she yelled, jumping into the fray. She grabbed two shirt collars and flung the boys back. The two other boys were on the ground with their victim. "I said, leave him alone!" she shouted. She managed to haul the small boy to his feet and set him behind her. As she faced the others, she realized with a thrill of fear that now she herself was in danger.

"Get out of here *now*," she said sternly. "I mean it." She wasn't sure her bluff would work, but she knew that she couldn't back down or show fear.

"You're lucky, lady . . . this time," the biggest boy said, jabbing a finger at her.

"Beat it." Heller hoped her shaking knees didn't show through her skirt. For a moment her gaze locked with the boy's, then he made a small gesture and the four disappeared down the street.

Heller turned and looked down at the dark-skinned boy she'd rescued. His ebony eyes were wide and frightened, and a trickle of blood oozed from the corner of his mouth. "Are you all right? Where do you live?"

The boy pointed and pulled on her skirt.

Heller was about to tell him that she couldn't go with him, that she had to get out of this dangerous area herself, but the pleading look in his eyes had her following him. They had walked only a block before the boy was leading her up the step of an old building, bright with a fresh coat of paint but in need of repair. Above the front door was a sign— PROMISE HOUSE. Heller had heard of this refuge for homeless children run by a Catholic priest. She turned to the boy. "Do you live here?" He didn't answer. She rang the bell, but the boy slipped around her and pushed the door open. They had no sooner stepped inside, when a tall man wearing a black suit and the familiar white collar walked down the hall toward them.

"How do you do? I'm Father Densmore. I see you've found Simeon."

"Does he live here?" Heller asked.

"You could say that. He is one of the few children here who comes from this area. He doesn't sleep here, but he comes to eat. I've been unable to learn much about his circumstances, so I don't feel I can turn him over to city authorities."

Heller had thought she'd leave right away, but instead followed the priest when he urged her to take a tour of the shabby brownstone.

"We house as many as we can, Miss Blane," Father Densmore said as they ended the tour in his office.

"I think you're doing admirable work, Father." Heller glanced at her watch. "Oh, I didn't realize it was so late. Do you mind if I use your phone to call my roommate, Father? She may be worried about me."

"Not at all. Be my guest."

Surreptitiously, she slipped all the quarters she had under the phone, then dialed. Doodie answered the phone on the first ring. "Hi, it's me. I just wanted to let you know I'm all right and I'll be home in a little bit . . . What? Con's there?" Her heart leapt that he had come to see her.

"What, Doodie? . . . Oh, he wants to come pick me up?" A vision of those four threatening boys flashed through her mind, and it suddenly seemed like a very good idea that Con come for her. "Well, okay, Doodie. Here's the address."

After she hung up, Heller turned to Father Densmore. "I have a ride. He should be here any moment."

"That's good," he said, "but I think Simeon will be sorry to see you go." She turned to the boy standing next to her and ran her hand over his almost bald head. She sent Father Densmore a questioning look.

He sighed. "I'm afraid his body was covered with nasty creatures and we had to shave his head. He's coming along." The priest smiled at the boy, who smiled back. "I think he may even talk to me one day."

"I don't think he's mute, and his hearing seems in order," Heller said.

"I think Simeon chooses not to speak. I'd guess the world hasn't been that friendly to him, so he deigns not to communicate with it."

On impulse, Heller pulled the boy close and hugged him, surprised when the thin arms came up and around her. She looked at the priest. "You said he doesn't sleep here, Father. May I take him with me? My roommate and I have plenty of room."

"Oh, my dear, you don't know what you'd be getting yourself into. Besides, Social Services would have to—"

"What good have they done Simeon? Let me take him, Father, if he wants to come with me." She turned to Simeon. "Do you have a family?"

The boy shook his head "no."

"Do you want to come stay with me for a while?"

He nodded enthusiastically.

"My friend works out of the apartment, and since I'm in the theater, I'll be home most days as well. We could care for him, find a tutor for him. We might help him, Father."

Father Densmore frowned. "Life has been cruel to Simeon."

"I wouldn't pick him up, then throw him away like an old shoe. Let me try, Father."

Heller went around and around with the priest, agreeing that he was right in all his arguments, but still not letting go. Somehow she knew she had to take Simeon with her, that it was the right thing to do. "You admit he doesn't really belong here, Father, that he's a street person. What difference would it make if I took him?"

"Rejecting him after giving him security would be the cruelest thing you could do to such a child."

"I know, Father, but—"

"Hi."

Heller whirled around, almost losing her balance. "Conrad!" Though it had been only a week since she'd last seen him, it might have been a year. Joy suffused her at the sight of him, an overwhelming sensation that all was right with the world. She felt that way each time she saw him. Things had a habit of sorting themselves out when Con was around.

She introduced Conrad to Father Densmore, aware

that Simeon kept his body pressed close to hers, as if he were afraid of this big stranger.

"And who is this?" Con asked, gazing down at Simeon.

"This is Simeon. I'm trying to convince Father Densmore that I can take care of him."

"What?" Con looked from the boy to her determined face. "I see." Conrad turned to the priest. "If I called my lawyer and had him talk to Social Services, would that ease your mind, Father?"

The priest sighed. "I don't like to put a spanner in the works, but your requests are irregular. We're going to have to look into this."

Con's lawyer worked wonders. He came right down to Promise House with reassuring evidence of Con's good citizenship and solid reputation. A paper was prepared for Father Densmore, then finally they were ready to leave.

Heller put her hand on the boy's head, and his sparse, tightly curled black hair tickled her palm. "Does he have clothes, Father? Or other belongings?"

"Just what's on his back." Father Densmore smiled at Simeon. "I will say this for him. Every day he goes down to our laundry and puts in his clothes, wearing an old discarded bathrobe until they're done."

"I think we can manage a shirt or two." She looked down at Simeon, who was gazing up at her. "Will you trust me to care for you, Simeon? Will you come home with me?" At his slow nod, her heart turned over. "Wait until you see Hector. He's my dog." A wary look entered his eyes, and she smiled. "And he happens to like boys very much. Okay?"

Simeon hesitated, then nodded.

Conrad leaned over and held out his right hand to Simeon. Simeon solemnly took his hand. "How would you like a ride in my car?"

The boy's eyes slipped from Con to Heller and back again, then he nodded once more.

"Good. Let's go. Thank you, Father. We'll be bringing Simeon to see you every other day as agreed." Con inclined his head toward Heller.

"Good-bye, Father," Heller said. "Thank you."

Con stepped back to let her precede him out of the office. As she passed him, he bent his head and let his mouth lightly caress her cheek. Air seemed trapped in her lungs as her entire body reacted to him, yearned for him. Outside he helped her into his Ferrari after Simeon had scrambled into the back. She felt his hand pass down her back all the way to her coccyx.

Simeon! She would concentrate on the boy. That would bring her heart back to normal rhythm.

As they drove south on Ninth Avenue, Heller kept looking over her shoulder at Simeon, happily curled up in the space behind the front seat.

"He'll be fine, you know," Conrad said.

"Why were you at the apartment? Didn't you have to work today?"

"Yes." He glanced at her. "I needed to see you. I'm sorry I haven't called for so long."

Seeing stars and planets, Heller tried to smile. "Thank you for coming to get me."

"What were you doing in such a dangerous area?"

"I was daydreaming and just wandered down the wrong streets."

"That's not very smart, Heller. How did you end up at Promise House?"

"Well . . . oh, I helped Simeon out of a little trouble, and he led me there."

"What the hell!" The car veered as Con glared at her. "What kind of 'little trouble'?"

"These kids were picking on him, and—"

"You involved yourself in a street fight?"

"They weren't very big, just bigger than Simeon."

"Dammit, Heller, you could have been hurt."

"I wasn't." She glanced back at Simeon. "I don't think we should argue. Simeon is looking distressed."

"And there's another thing you might not have thought of, Heller. How do you expect to care for the boy with a job?"

"Rehearsals end in a week. Once the show starts, I'll only have to perform in two weekly matinees and rehearse maybe twice a week. That'll leave me plenty of time to spend with Simeon."

The closer they got to the Village, the greater was Heller's concern about Doodie's reaction to Simeon. She knew Doodie had a heart of gold and was a soft touch for any stray, but Simeon was a little different from your average abandoned kitten.

Con parked the car and they all got out. As they neared the warehouse, Simeon clutched Heller's hand and dug in his heels.

"Don't worry, Simeon," she said softly, gazing into his big black eyes. "I'm coming with you. I live here."

"And I'm coming in too," Con said, holding out his hand to Simeon.

There was a pregnant pause, then the boy put his other hand into Con's. His breathing increased audibly as they stepped into the cavernous building and took the elevator up to the second floor.

Doodie came out of her studio, her paint-daubed smock looking like a kaleidoscope, her hands busily wiping a brush on a cloth. "Goodness, company. Excuse the outfit, folks. Next time I'll be in a tux.

Hello again, Con. Who is this?" She hunkered down so that she was face-to-face with Simeon.

"I've brought him home to live with us," Heller said.

Doodie looked up but didn't move from her position in front of the boy. "Oh. I wish I'd known. I think it's going to be bologna sandwiches for dinner. I didn't get to the store."

"I'll go buy some food," Con said. "And please don't protest, Heller. After all, I did help you bring him here." He smiled at her, then left the apartment.

"He could make any woman's heart go pitty-pat," Doodie said musingly.

"Or head go thump-thump." Heller inhaled a deep breath. "It's your place, Doodie. If you mind about . . ." She inclined her head toward Simeon.

"I don't mind at all. I can't tell you how lonely this place has been. Now all in one fell swoop we're a family. Leonard will love Simeon."

Heller hugged her friend. "I hope I won't have to fight you for him."

"You might. Come on, Simeon. Let's look at your sleeping quarters."

Simeon didn't budge until Heller told him she'd go with him. Heller's section of the apartment was big and airy. Next to her bedroom was a good-sized storage area that would suit Simeon perfectly. It even had two large windows that actually opened with no more than two tugs.

"We can clean it after dinner," Doodie said enthusiastically. "And that foldaway bed I have will be perfect for him."

Back in the kitchen Doodie poured three glasses of lemonade. When she turned she saw Simeon staring in fascination at the paintbrushes in her voluminous smock pocket.

"Take them all, Simeon. Tomorrow I'll show you a spot in my studio where you can use them."

His smile was slow in coming, but when it arrived it enthralled the two women watching him.

Half an hour later they heard the elevator doors clank open, then a bumping noise. They walked out into the entry area to see Con standing there with a load of groceries.

"My Lord, Con," Heller said. "Did you have to buy out the store?"

While she and Doodie put the food away, Con sat at the kitchen table beside Simeon.

"Will you tell me what you think of your new home, Simeon?" he asked softly. Simeon shook his head.

"Can he speak?" Doodie whispered to Heller.

"It would seem he doesn't choose to do so."

"Oh. Well, people talk too much anyway. C'mon, Simeon, I know there are apples in the refrigerator. I'd like one. How about you?"

His slow nod was followed by a hand reaching up to Doodie. She smiled tearily as she took it.

"I can see that Simeon has won over your friend," Con said. He turned to Heller. "You're pale. Are you sure this boy won't be too much for you?"

She shook her head. "I am grateful for all you did for us today."

He shook off her gratitude. "Let me put a chauffeur at your disposal until you're fully recovered."

"Thanks, but I really am recovered. I either walk or take a subway to the theater, and—"

"I insist that you let me see to Simeon's transportation back and forth to Promise House each day."

Heller didn't need any more reasons to be ensnared by Con. She loved him too much already. Now he was being so good about Simeon, drawing her even closer to him. "Thank you."

"Little devil," Con said affectionately. "Someday we'll talk about that macabre sense of humor of yours."

"Will we now?"

"Oh, yes, indeed we will." He leaned down to kiss her nose, then turned and walked toward the elevator.

"Con, aren't you going to stay and eat with us?"

He swung around to face her, his head cocked to one side. "Do you know that's the first time you've initiated anything between us since I found you in Barbados? I would like to eat with you."

"You did buy the food," Heller said impishly.

"So I did. I've also arranged for a delivery of food each day. A growing boy needs sustenance."

"Still managing my life?"

"Trying," he said dryly, holding out his hand to her. "Shall we begin preparing dinner?"

"Ah, yes, I suppose we could do that." As usual, he'd thrown her off stride, she thought. She was torn between wanting to kiss him and kill him. The man was lethal. With a crook of his finger he could call her to his side. It wasn't good to let him get too close. If the Domini brothers ever found her, Conrad himself might be in danger.

When she and her mother had been put in the witness protection program almost four years before, they had been assured that Bruno Domini and his brother Anthony would never find them. They were relocated, given new names, new pasts, and the paper trail left behind them was destroyed. Still, in all this time Heller had never been able to shake her fear that somehow the Domini brothers would find her. It was bad enough that Doodie—who knew the whole story—was in danger simply by living with her. And now Simeon. But she couldn't believe even the Dominis would hurt either of them. But Con was a different matter. If he became a permanent part of her life, he would definitely be at risk . . . No, she couldn't do that.

"Don't try to erect walls between us," he said. "It won't work."

She glared at him. "Quit reading my mind." She whirled and started for the kitchen.

He caught her and kissed her hard on the mouth. "I like kissing you, Heller Blane."

"We have to fix dinner."

"There's that squeak in your voice again."

He followed her into the kitchen, admiring the graceful sway of her body. Her tall, lissome figure was totally sensual and exciting. He wanted her as badly as he had the first night he'd seen her, darting from table to table in the bar of the Andre. But as much as he wanted her, craved her, he knew it was wise to hold off becoming her lover again. Although he was certain Heller loved him, he also realized she felt constrained to keep him at arm's length. He would go along with her for now, but as soon as he figured out what the problem was and had dealt with it, he'd have her back in his bed in an instant.

"You move beautifully, Heller," he said. "I can still recall cupping your wonderful bare derriere in my hands."

"Conrad!"

"You're a great temptation, darling."

"Why don't you wash these vegetables?" she said shakily. "I'll go see how hungry Doodie and Simeon are."

She escaped from the kitchen, trying to stop her heart from pounding against her ribs. She followed the sound of Doodie's voice to her studio. "Hey, you two, what's up?"

"Heller, come here and look at the way he draws." Doodie shot a glance behind Heller. "Did the Big, the Bad, and the Beautiful leave?"

"No," Heller said abruptly, leaning down to look at the shaky outline of an animal Simeon had drawn. "That's a very good elephant, Simeon. Have you been to the zoo?" He shook his head, and she patted his cheek. "Well, we're going one day. Sundays the zoo is too crowded. But school will be out soon and we'll have the time."

"I think I'll go too," Doodie said, grimacing at the mountain of sketches strewn around the room.

Heller laughed. Her friend was constantly fighting the battle of the deadline.

"Does he know, Heller?"

Heller understood at once what her friend was referring to, and she whipped her head toward the door. No one was there. She looked back at Doodie. "No. You're the only person on earth who has any idea about my past . . . I think."

"Why don't you tell Con?"

Heller shook her head. "It's all over now." If only she could believe that, she thought. "It was a rough three years, but now they can't touch my mother. The death notice of Mona Terrence was in the Syracuse paper. Her testimony is on record, What else could they want?"

"You. And you know that's true. Revenge with those people is a way of life."

"There's no point in doing anything to me now. I never knew—" Heller saw Doodie stiffen and stopped talking at once. Turning slowly, she saw a smiling Con standing in the doorway. Were his eyes a shade harder, she wondered. Was she imagining that there was a wiry tension to him, as though he were re-straining a wild animal?

"Ladies, Simeon, we will have our dinner in about an hour. Would you mind if I went home and changed? I think I would be more comfortable out of this suit."

"You fixed dinner for us?" Doodie beamed. "Sure, go home and change, but hurry back."

"I will. You can be assured of that." His gaze ran lazily up and down Heller's body. "See you soon."

When he left, Heller sagged against the wall. Had he overheard the conversation with Doodie?

Con place a phone call from his car as he drove home. Although he lived on the east side of Manhattan and Heller in the southwest, it didn't take him long to get home. He needed to return to Heller as quickly as possible, and that urgency drove him.

He parked in the underground garage of his building and stepped out of the car. Immediately he sensed someone was hiding, waiting for him. It had been years since Vietnam, but his sense of survival had been honed sharp and was still part of him. Crouching with his back to the car, he headed for the protection of shadows.

"Nice countermove, Mr. W. I thought I had you."

"Tabor! Is that you? Dammit, man, why didn't you identify yourself?"

"Checking on your readiness, Mr. W. You sent for me?"

"Yes. I didn't expect you here this quickly. I just called from my car a few minutes ago."

"Beeper," Tabor said. "I was only a block away, so

I decided to visit. Sounds like you have a handle on something strange."

"I don't know, but I overheard a conversation that . . . intrigued me." Con repeated what he'd heard Heller say to Doodie, including her mother's name, Mona Terrence. "I thought it sounded like a witness protection program thing. What do you think?"

"Could be. If this person thinks she's safe from people who have dogged her, she could be mighty wrong. If it's the mob, she can't bank on anything. Those people have ways of finding things out."

"Get on it, will you, Tabor? I need the full picture, and quickly. Expense is no problem."

Tabor gave Con a flip salute and disappeared into the shadows. "Expect to hear from me in a day or so."

The voice drifted out of the darkness to Con but he barely heard it. His concentration was on Heller. Cold perspiration ran over him at the thought that she might be tied into the mob for any reason. Dammit, he wouldn't have it!

When he reached his apartment he gazed around the impeccably furnished living room. Not for the first time he felt a loneliness here. He had counted on Heller staying with him, and the fact that she wasn't had put a hole in his existence that was alien and uncomfortable. One of these days—and soon—he was going to fix that.

The next day Con was at the warehouse apartment very early. He was about to ring the bell, when he noticed that the outside door was ajar. Frowning, he pushed it open and walked in. When the elevator doors opened on the second floor, he could hear voices. He paused a moment to catch the direction, then ambled toward the kitchen. His footsteps were muffled by the strip of carpet that ran down the center of the floor.

"But what if you should be hassled by those people, Heller? You and Simeon would be safer here."

"Thanks, friend. I appreciate the offer, but when you and Leonard are married, you'll need this space for yourselves." Heller took a deep breath. "Besides, if I do have to face . . . the other thing, I may be leaving Simeon with you."

"Don't you say that, Heller Blane. It would be better if you stayed here. We have a lot of protection. Hector is very good. Look how close he is to Simeon already."

Con looked down at the big dog who was licking his hand, and he shook his head. Unlocked door . . . friendly dog. Some protection! But whatever protection Heller needed, he would supply the armor to shield her.

Tabor had called him that morning.

"You were right, Mr. W.," he'd said. "It looks like Miss Blane has been in the WPP for a few years. Her mother, Mona Terrence, was an accountant for a construction firm called the Domini Brothers. It's an upstate outfit. They were undercutting their jobs, pocketing the differences. Mona Terrence was a real scrapper. She blew the whistle on them and she and her daughter were put into the witness protection program. Their tracks were well-covered, but a few months ago there was an obituary in the Syracuse paper for Mona Terrence. She'd died of a heart attack."

"I see." So that was Heller's secret, Con had thought. "Keep digging . . . and thanks." Anger at the unknown Domini brothers who threatened his lady had filled Con. Already he was planning what he could do. Heller's voice brought him out of his reverie.

"Doodie, you're crazy."

"I don't want you to leave, Heller."

"Why don't we wait until Leonard comes and then discuss it with him?"

"He'll agree with me. You know how he feels about you." Doodie paused. "I could tie you to a chair, but you'd miss your rehearsals then."

"True. You're a nut, Doodie Kleinfeltz."

"Yeah. We're a team, Heller. Swear you won't leave until we've exhausted the alternatives."

"Cross my heart and hope to die."

"You know, Simeon really enjoyed dinner last night. I think he likes Con. I know I do."

"The man's a giant magnet," Heller said dryly. "Now, remember. Simeon has a class at Promise House this morning. Do you mind getting him up?"

"Of course not. I can't wait to see what he looks like in those clothes we bought him."

"Only you would know a children's clothes designer with leftovers."

"Sam's a good designer and his business is growing. I knew he would have something."

"I wish I could stay to see him, but I have a checkup at the hospital this morning. It'll take me a while to get there, so I have to leave in about ten minutes. I know the doctor's going to find me in great shape. I've been feeling better each day, and I think the dance rehearsals have helped."

"You won't have to leave so soon," Con said. He stepped into the kitchen and the two women gaped at him.

"How did you get in here?" Heller asked. "I didn't hear the bell."

"I didn't ring it because the door was open." He petted Hector, who was gamboling around him. "Your watchdog was just showing me where the good silver is."

Doodie winced. "His training might take a little longer."

"A lot longer, I would say," Con drawled, grinning.

"Actually, Hector is getting better." Heller's look dared Con to deny it.

"The next step would be to teach him to close the downstairs door."

"Damn, I'm always doing that when I go out for a paper," Doodie said. "Would you like some coffee, Con?"

"I'd love some. Actually, I brought breakfast with me." He took from a bag golden flaky croissants and imported jams and marmalades and set then on the table.

"Ummm, that looks good," Doodie said. "I'll pour the coffee."

"Shall we sit down?" Con saw the look of concern on Heller's face and surmised that she was trying to decide if he had overheard her and Doodie.

"Thanks for bringing all this, Con," she said, "but I don't have time to eat. I have to catch a bus. . . ."

"No, you don't. I'm driving you to the hospital, and I've arranged for a car to take Simeon to Promise House and back."

"Thank you." Heller smiled uncertainly, then turned to Doodie. "I'll be able to see Simeon in his new clothes."

"And I'll be more comfortable about him going to Promise House." Doodie grinned at Con as she handed him a steaming cup of coffee.

"Thank you, Doodie." Con smiled at the woman, then raised his brows as Simeon, rubbing his eyes and yawning, stumbled into the kitchen. "Good morning, Simeon. Come and have some breakfast."

Heller jumped up and hurried to the small stove, where a pan of scrambled eggs was steaming.

Doodie moved up behind her. "He could charm the fleas off a dog," she muttered.

"True." Heller remembered how absolutely beguiling he could be . . . in bed. "Ouch." Sticking her burned finger in her mouth, she castigated herself for being a fool.

"You shouldn't have grabbed that without a mitt," Con said from behind her. "Were you daydreaming?"

"Something like that," she mumbled, running cold water over her hand. She whisked the pan off the stove and served the eggs. "Here we are, Simeon. Eggs for everybody. Do you like grape juice?" At the boy's nod Heller smiled and gestured to the vitamin pills next to his glass. "Take those to give you strong bones."

"I'll have some too, Mommy," Con said. He was feeling a pinch of irritation at all the attention Heller was lavishing on the boy.

"All right, baby." Heller laughed and made a move at him.

Before she could move away, he reached up and kissed her. Heller pulled back, her heart thumping, ready to sting him with words until she heard the childish laughter. She stared at Simeon.

Con lowered his cup slowly. "Well, well," Con said. "So you have a sense of humor, do you?"

Simeon's mirthful eyes turned his way and his smile widened, his mustache of orange marmalade moving upward.

"Since we have two women to care for, Simeon, we'll need a sense of humor." Con pretended to duck as the two women rounded on him. The boy's laughter increased.

Simeon sobered abruptly, though, when he saw Doodie and Heller fumble for tissues to wipe their eyes. He gazed questioningly at Con.

"Ladies often cry when they're happy, Simeon," Con said gently. His own throat tightened when the boy's smile turned on again.

"Now run along and brush your teeth," Heller said as Simeon finished the last of his eggs. "You need to go soon."

After Simeon left, Con set down his coffee and turned to Heller. "Did I tell you that I've decided to have a dress rehearsal party to raise money for Promise House?"

"No, you didn't," Heller said faintly. "Won't you have to discuss that with the producer, Mr. Dumont?"

Con shrugged. "I don't see any problem. Aeneas Dumont is a friend of mine. I'll call him this morning. Don't you think Promise House could use the money?"

"Oh, yes," Heller answered distractedly. Despite her delight at Con's generous act, she was still mulling over the conversation she'd been having with Doodie when he'd arrived. Could he have heard anything?

Five

The dress rehearsal was going well, with remarkably few hitches. Many of the songs were memorable toe-tappers, and the glitzy, high-class audience had enthusiastically applauded each one. The play could have a long run.

During intermission Con paced the lobby.

"Brother dear," his sister Ione said. "I understand that the girl of your dreams is in the second act. I'm dying to see her."

"Are you? And how did you find out about Heller?"

"Mother wheedled it out of Dad, then couldn't keep it to herself. How long have you known . . ." Ione glanced at her playbill. "Heller Blane? I love the name, but it's very theatrical."

"It's her own," Con said tartly. "And I've known her for some time. There's the signal for the end of intermission."

"Saved by the bell." Ione tucked her hand in his

arm. "I'm not at all displeased by this. You've turned human on me. Skittish about her debut?"

"Yes."

"What will Natalie Dixon do when she finds out you're not on her string anymore? Ah, you have that satirical look again. Maybe you didn't think you were Natalie's, but she did."

"Then she's wrong," he said abruptly.

"Mother invited her and her family this evening."

"Not at my request. I asked her to use the *intimate* list, and she went and filled every seat in the orchestra."

"Everyone loves it, though. This may be a hit. Do you have a piece of it?"

"Now I do."

Everybody took their seats and slowly the rustling ceased. The curtain opened on a pivotal scene, in which the ingenue lead would go to a theater and discover that her big sister was a stripper.

The stage was set with tables and chairs around a runway such as models parade along in a fashion show. The lights were dim, and the people onstage were all rough, coarse-looking men. The ingenue entered the strip joint and endured some heckling from the other patrons as she desperately looked for her sister. Abruptly, the orchestra began playing a bawdy, suggestive tune. An emcee jumped up on the runway and announced, "And here she is, Honey, the star of our show!" The audience on the stage and in the seats went motionless.

A spotlight centered on the bottom of a curtain at the far end of the runway. Slowly the curtain parted to reveal a tall blonde completely wrapped in a shimmering white cape. With a sensual, hip-swiveling walk, she moved forward. The spangles and sequins on her high-collared cape glittered in the spotlight as it rose from her feet to her face.

Con gasped. "Dammit!" It was Heller. She had been hired to play the part of a stripper!

When she was halfway down the runway, she began to sing a compelling song, enticing all men to come to her and love her, worship her. Con was awed by the range and timbre of her voice. Though it didn't have the slick, well-trained sound of the rest of the cast, it seemed to invade the theater like a hot, sinuous promise. Throbbing, her voice clung to each person as she slinked and slithered, step by slow step, to the end of the runway. When her song ended, the onstage audience cheered and whistled, and she started to dance.

As her body alternately swayed and jerked in a blatantly sexual rhythm, she coyly parted her voluminous cape, revealing a nearly naked body before quickly closing it again. She teased and taunted both audiences, carefully sidestepping the eager hands that grabbed for her high-heeled sequined sandals as she flashed various parts of her body. From what Con could see, her tiny costume was backless, and slit in front to below her navel. Her breasts were barely covered, and as for the lower part of her body . . . She wouldn't be arrested, but he wasn't sure he'd make it till the end of her number.

At last, as the music reached a crescendo and Con thought he would explode, she dropped the cape and, with one last sensual slither, stood motionless, her legs apart, her head back, her arms reaching for the stars.

Applause rose like a thunderous wave, crashing over the stage, startling some of the performers and stunning Heller. Again and again she bowed before she left the stage.

"Very nice, brother," Ione whispered, leaning toward Con. "I'm glad I came."

"That's enough, Ione," her husband, Will, said, pulling her back into her seat.

"Darling, are you grinding your teeth?" Con's mother asked. "Oh, dear, I thought you'd outgrown that."

"Shh!" Con's father admonished everyone.

The play continued rapidly to its happy musical ending. The long, boisterous applause at its finish delighted all the performers.

Backstage, wearing a robe, Heller stood clustered with the other actors who had had minor parts. She was surprised when more and more people stopped to congratulate her.

"My dear," said one woman as she shook her hand. "I must say that I was not delighted when my son asked me to help organize this evening, but it has been wonderful. You gave a stellar performance, infusing your part with a verve and excitement that makes it memorable. I predict you will be a hit."

"Thank you." Heller gazed at the tall, slender, soignée woman. They had never met, but even if the woman hadn't mentioned "her son," Heller would have recognized her as Con's mother. They had the same emerald eyes.

"Hello, Heller," Con said, appearing beside his mother, a man who was an older version of himself at his side. "I'd like to introduce you to my parents, Melanie and Simon Wendel. May I present Heller Blane."

Heller caught the tight, controlled way he was speaking and stared at him. Con was angry. She'd been afraid this would happen. She smiled at his parents. "How do you do?"

"Quite well, thank you," Melanie Wendel said. "I applaud how fully you've recovered from your injuries, Heller. Your dancing proves you're in fine shape. Con has told us how brave you were, rescuing those children. It was wonderful."

"Indeed it was." Simon Wendel shook her hand. "I thought you might be coming to work for us again, but as much as I'm sure you would do a good job, tonight you showed your prowess as a performer."

"Indeed you did." Ione stepped around her father and clutched Heller's hand. "I thought Con was going to choke. I'm his sister Ione, by the way."

Melanie studied Con. "Surely he wasn't *choking.*"

"Everything is fine, Mother." Con glared at his sister, but she just smiled unrepentingly.

Heller looked at the four Wendels and couldn't restrain the chuckle that rose in her.

"What's so funny?" Con asked, moving close to her, effectively blocking her from the rest of the room.

"You, your family." She laughed out loud.

"You won't always have the protection of a crowd, Heller."

Poking her tongue out at him was an impulse she couldn't control, and if Con hadn't leaned toward her at the same moment, it wouldn't have mattered. But a flash went off and Heller wanted to sink.

Con shielded her with his body and looked over his shoulder at the photographer. "Give me that damned camera."

The photographer measured the distance to the door and jumped for it. However, Will, Con's brother-in-law, intercepted him. "Sorry, old man. Mustn't take such unflattering pictures of the performers. Let me reimburse you for the film." Will took his camera, opened it, and pulled the film out. "There." He pressed some bills into the hapless man's hands. "Remember to take more flattering poses next time."

"Don't worry." The man glared at them and left.

"Shall we move on to the restaurant?" Con asked. "You must be starving." His gaze was riveted on Heller as her robe parted slightly in the front, revealing her skimpy costume. Her long, shapely legs were more sexy than ever as the wispy feathers attached to the costume brushed against her thighs. He could see her flat stomach contract and expand with each breath. "Get dressed!" he said abruptly. "I'll wait for you."

"There's no need to—"

"Heller!"

"I was trying to say that I'm waiting for Simeon and Doodie."

"I've already arranged for them to go to the restaurant with my parents. I didn't think you'd want them to walk."

"But Simeon was looking forward to seeing me after the show." His high-handedness was once more making her temper bubble.

"Not like that. God!" He pulled her robe closed as it again gapped open. "I'm going to buy you a proper robe. Why in hell did you take this part?"

"Because it was offered to me, the pay is good, and I'm enjoying myself."

"That damned outfit is cut to the navel."

"Right. I'm supposed to be a stripper."

Con pivoted and stormed out of the backstage area.

Heller muttered to herself all the while she washed

and changed. It felt so good to have the stage makeup off her face that she settled for using only a tinted moisturizer, pale lip gloss, and a touch of mascara.

Her silk dress was the mysterious color of the Caribbean Sea, and the sheer material whirled about her when she walked. She flicked a brush through her short curly hair, straightened her shoulders, and opened the dressing room door.

Con had been slouched against the opposite wall. He straightened when he saw her, and his gaze roved over every inch of her. "That aqua color turns your eyes to a true turquoise. Where's your coat?"

"It's a warm spring evening. I don't need one."

He took her arm and led her from the theater, pausing when she said good night to the guard at the backstage door. "Found yourself a home, haven't you?" His words were sharp.

"Not really, but I do like the stage and feel I was lucky to get the job." She paused. "Thanks to you and Manny Levin."

"I'm hoist by my own petard." Con helped her into his car, which sat in a no-parking zone next to the theater. "You were sensational and you know it."

"You must get a great many parking tickets," she said as he gunned the engine.

"Actually, I don't. Usually I'm a model citizen."

"Hah!"

"That's sounds a bit unkind."

"As though you cared what other people think."

"I value your opinion so much that I was willing to make you a special assistant to the head of Wendel International."

"That's you?"

"Yes."

"That smacks of—of nepotism, or something."

"You're not my relative."

"But your staff would have been offended."

"I doubt it."

"You sound unctuous."

"Do I?"

"Yes, and now you sound miffed."

"Why hasn't anyone strangled you by this time?"

"Actually, I'm a model citizen."

Con was torn between ire and humor. When his laugh burst from him, Heller turned her head and looked at him. "Why are you staring, darling? Were you expecting something else?"

"A karate chop, a haymaker, an uppercut maybe? You're unpredictable."

They drove only a few blocks through the crowded theater district. When the car stopped, Heller stared at the front of the famous restaurant. "Sardi's! I've always wanted to come here, but thought I'd have to wait until I was a star."

He kissed her as he helped her from the car. "You are a star."

Heller had the feeling that she'd been maneuvered into a corner somehow and that Con was moving into that corner with her. How simple it would be to let him. But what did she know of his feelings for her? He might seem possessive of her, but he hadn't told her he loved her since their one night together at the Andre in New York. Nor had he done any more than lightly kiss her since that night in her apartment two weeks ago. Did he perhaps just feel responsible for her in some strange way?

"Shall we go in?" he asked, interrupting her thoughts. "I'm sure the rest of the cast is inside and ready to devour the tablecloths."

Pandemonium hit them when the door was opened.

The entire large main floor of the restaurant was packed with noisy, laughing people.

"The sound of success," Con whispered in her ear. "The cast is on a high."

Rather than try to answer in the din, Heller nodded her head, feeling some of the excitement enter her.

"Heller darling! There you are! I've been waiting for you." Carleton Desmond, the director, swept her into his arms and kissed her on the mouth. "*You* were a smash!" he shouted. "This was a very fussy audience, and they loved the play and you."

"Thank you, Desi." Heller tried to smile at him, but she was too busy watching Con. His face seemed carved from granite and his eyes were glittering with enmity. "Oh, Desi, someone is calling you."

Con took hold of her arm and began leading her away. "We're over here."

"Will you stop acting like Attila the Hun? Desi kisses everyone like that."

"Does he?"

"Yes. Now let me g—" She bit off her words as they reached his family's table.

"Do come and sit next to me, Heller," Melanie said. "I want to hear all about you."

Con saw her stiffen at his mother's words, saw her eyes shift as she glanced nervously over her shoulder. Was she thinking of the Domini brothers?

"Who is that awkward, ungainly child?" The high-pitched, cultured voice cut through all the other noise. It seemed that everyone in the room turned to look at the young black boy just about to put a pâté-laden cracker into his mouth. "Should he be here?"

"For God's sake, Natalie, " Desi said, "keep your voice down."

"Why should I, darling? I gave a great deal of money to be at this party."

"Damn the bitch," Con said softly. He started to move toward the stricken boy, but an angry blonde in an aqua-blue dress streaked by him.

Everyone watched as Heller, her face tight with fury, picked up a champagne glass and flung its contents at Natalie Dixon, socialite and sometime backer of plays.

"He's mine," Heller announced in a deadly voice. "And don't you ever try to belittle him again. I won't allow it."

"Oh, dear," Doodie whispered to Con's family. "Heller's having one of her hissy fits. No one should mess with her right now. That poor woman didn't know that Heller always takes care of her own."

To add insult to injury, Simeon tromped down on Natalie's toe, and Natalie's screeching soprano went up an octave.

"That . . . does . . . it, Carleton." Natalie turned on the director, who was staring admiringly at Heller. "You either throw her and her changeling out of the show or I withdraw." She drew in a deep breath and stared angrily at those who dared to titter. But she was even more furious at the people who were ignoring her and already attacking the buffet table.

Con stepped forward, his hand pressing warningly on Heller's arm when it looked as though she would say more. "I would be glad to buy your piece in the play, Natalie. Name your price."

She glared at him. "I'm not selling. I just want that trollop out of the show and out of here."

"Dictating policy in a play? I should think the

producer and director would hate that. The offer still goes, but I can tell you now that I have enough shares in the show to buck you on this." He smiled, but his eyes were hard.

"As do I," Con's father said softly, standing at his son's side.

Natalie dramatically gathered her cloak around herself. "I'll sue."

"So will I," Con said in a deceptively mild voice, "if the show doesn't go on just as is."

Natalie seemed to swell, then she tossed her head and swept past them and out of the restaurant.

"Shall we eat?" Melanie asked. "I'm feeling rather peckish." She smiled at Simeon. "Come along, Simeon. You shall escort me to the buffet table. Would you do that for me?"

Simeon hesitated, glancing at both Doodie and Heller. They nodded and very shyly he stretched up his hand to Melanie. She took it and he smiled.

"Come along, Doodie," Simon said. "You shall be my partner."

Left alone, Con grinned at Heller. "Did you have to throw the champagne down the front of her dress? It had been well chilled and was at a perfect temperature for drinking."

"She needed something to cool her down, the hussy. Her dress was cut lower than my costume." Heller glared in the direction of the exit.

"But she doesn't have your beautiful breasts, darling."

Heller rounded on him. "And I suppose you've seen hers?"

"Heller, how you talk. Let's eat, shall we?"

"You didn't answer me," she muttered to Con's back as he walked away. By the time they were heading back to their table with laden plates, she was seething with jealousy. "Roué!" She whispered harshly as he pulled out her chair.

For a moment he looked nonplused, than he smiled. "I'm beginning to understand that convoluted mind of yours. Still miffed that I might have looked at Natalie's glorious breasts."

"You said they weren't as good as mine," she snapped, then groaned when he grinned.

"They aren't, my sweet, I assure you. No one's could be."

"Don't try to weasel out of this, you—you bluebeard."

"Bluebeard?" Ione repeated as they sat down. "Whatever have you done now, Con? I'm agog."

"Dear sister, put a sock in it."

"Con," Melanie chided, "must you use such expressions? It sounds so discordant."

Heller sensed Con's ire and it was a balm to her spirit. "I couldn't agree more. English is quite beautiful when spoken properly."

Melanie smiled at Heller. "Very astute of you, my dear."

"Heller's an apple polisher," Con drawled. "She's just trying to get on the good side of her mother-in-law-to-be." He smiled lazily as Heller sputtered and her face reddened. "Pulled your cork, didn't I, darling?"

"There you go again, Con," his mother said. "Isn't there another way you could have expressed yourself?"

"I'll try, Mother."

"I do hope you can cure that weakness in Con before you have children, Heller. I should hate my grandchildren to talk in such a way. Is something wrong, dear? Did you swallow something the wrong way? Pat her on the back, Con."

"With the greatest of pleasure." Con tapped her none too gently between the shoulder blades. "Better?"

"Monster!" Heller choked out, and grabbed for a glass of ice water.

"Heller must have gotten a crumb of bread in her throat, Mother," Con said, quickly removing the glass from her hand when she adjusted it to throwing position.

"Be careful, Heller," Melanie said. "You mustn't eat too fast. But I'm certainly glad you enjoy your food."

"When is the great event to be?" Ione asked.

"Soon."

"Never."

Heller and Con spoke at the same time. She glared at him while he smiled back.

"Make up your mind. I would like to give Heller a shower."

"Good idea, Ione. Do it as soon as possible."

Heller was still furious when Desi approached their table. "Dance, Heller?"

"I'd love to." She jumped to her feet, glad to get away from the silken net that was Con and his family.

"My, you do have influential friends, love," Desi said as they walked to the small area that had been cleared for dancing.

She clutched his shoulder as he swung her around in time to the music. "Don't be too impressed. I'm nothing to the Wendels."

Carleton Desmond laughed and held her closer. "Don't tell me that. The crown prince of Wendel hasn't taken his eyes off you since we got here."

"Don't be foolish."

"He hasn't, and since he and his papa will be

sinking more money into the play, I don't think you should back away from the relationship."

"Don't be a twit, Desi, and mind your own business. I like being in the show, but I won't play any of your little games."

Desi laughed. "Independent, aren't you? All right, Heller, have it your way. How would it be if I just moved in on the Great One's territory? Think he'd mind?"

Before she could respond, he pressed his mouth against hers, trying to force his tongue between her lips. Surprise kept her mobile for a second, then she jerked free of him.

At the same instant she felt herself being lifted and put to one side. She twisted around to see Con, his face contorted with rage. His father and brother-in-law were right behind him.

"She's mine, Desmond," Con said harshly. "Stay away from her and out of our lives. I won't tell you again."

"Cool your jets," Desi retorted. "Backing a play gives you no rights with the players. Not the kind you want, at any rate."

Open-mouthed, Heller watched Con's well-muscled body gather itself. Before she could make a sound he swung one sinewed arm. His fist connected with Desi's jaw, sending the man sprawling.

The other people in the room began shouting, jumping from their seats to watch the two men.

Will and Simon tried to get between them, but they were pushed away. The combatants were intent only on each other.

As Desi threw a punch at Con, flashbulbs went off. Appalled, Heller turned, and was immediately blinded as a photographer took her picture. She looked back at Con and Desi, who were circling each other like contenders in a boxing ring, eager to tangle.

Stepping between them, she glared first at one, then the other. "Stop for just a moment. I am going home now. Once I'm gone, you two can carry on with your silly jousting. Good-bye."

"I like that girl,", she heard Simon say to Will as she stalked away. "She has grit."

Without a backward look, she collected Doodie and Simeon, nodded to Melanie and Ione, and strode from the restaurant. Con stood in the center of the room, Desi forgotten, his eyes on the departing trio.

Heller was up early the next day, moving quietly so as not to disturb Simeon. Her eyes felt sticky and heavy, and her muscles ached.

A shower helped to dispel some of the cobwebs of a sleepless night, spent alternately cursing Con and Desi. Dressed in sweats, she put on the coffee, then jogged to the small neighborhood grocery store. She picked up a half gallon of milk and orange juice—Simeon went through both as if there were a run on the market—freshly baked croissants, and the paper.

Back at the apartment, she poured herself a cup of coffee and sat down to read the morning news. It was while she was spreading cherry jam on a croissant that she noticed the headline. "Party at Sardi's Turns into Brawl over Actress."

She dropped the croissant as she stared at the accompanying photograph. "Oh, no! Damn Con Wendel and his temper. I look like a fish out of water."

"Who looks like a fish?" Doodie asked. She yawned as she sat down beside Heller.

"I do." Heller pushed the paper toward her.

"Holy cow, Heller. Your mouth is hanging open so wide you could drive a car through."

"Thank you. It needed only that." She folded her arms on the table and dropped her head on them.

"Don't cry, Heller. I didn't mean to hurt your feelings."

"I'm not crying. I'm planning a murder . . . Con Wendel's."

"Oh, I don't know. I think his picture is kind of cute. That bear look is so macho."

"Don't simper, Doodie. It isn't—what? What picture? I didn't see any."

"See, right next to the doorman who's trying to get him out of there."

"Good Lord!" Heller stared at the two angry men. "Maybe no one will recognize him."

"I don't think that's too likely, since his mother and sister and father are in one of the pictures too."

"Worse and worse," Heller muttered. "Damn Con. I could lose my job because of this."

"Naw. It's good publicity. People like brawls."

"This people doesn't."

"I think people is plural not singular."

The phone rang before Heller could respond.

Still yawning, Doodie rose from her chair and picked up the receiver. "Hello? Yes, she's here. Would you like to talk—"

Heller turned around to see her friend staring at the phone. "Who is it?"

"It was someone for you, but he hung up." Doodie's eyes widened as she realized the implications. "No, don't look like that, Heller. It couldn't be any of those people."

"Why not? I understand their power reaches everywhere."

"Your mom is dead. Those men went to prison. That company was too small to interest the more powerful underworld."

"That's what I've told myself over and over, but there's always that little voice . . ."

"Don't think like that, Heller. Look how long it blighted life for you and your mom. Her death was the end of it."

Heller took a deep breath and nodded slowly.

"And," Doodie went on, "I hope that's not what's keeping you from that hunk, Con Wendel."

Heat rushed through Heller, leaving her strangely cold. "He's . . . I can't involve him in something that could be dangerous. I shouldn't even be living here with you."

Doodie's laugh seemed to lift the heavy air in the room. "Sorry, Heller. Believe me. I'm not denigrating what's happened. It's just that I can't imagine any situation too dangerous for Conrad Wendel."

Heller couldn't keep from smiling. "He is like an eighteen wheeler at times."

"Would you believe an aircraft carrier at full speed?" Doodie walked back to the table and hugged Heller. "Don't let him get away. His kind come one to a customer, once in a lifetime, just like my Leonard."

"Leonard is no battering ram."

"And Con Wendel is. Give up, friend, and grab the guy."

"You're charging full steam ahead as usual, Doodie."

"You bet. By the way, I left Simeon in the shower. I'll bet that whippet will have taken all the hot water." She sprinted from the room, leaving Heller with the paper and its picture of Con.

* * *

Half an hour later, as Heller was finishing slicing a melon for breakfast, the downstairs buzzer sounded. Surprised, she looked at her watch as she walked toward the intercom by the elevator. Seven-thirty! Who could be at the door so early?

She pressed the intercom button. "Yes?"

"Open the door, Heller. It's Con."

She opened her mouth to tell him to disappear, but the implacable note in his voice gave her pause. "It's very early and we have to get Simeon—"

"I know all that. I'll see to it that the boy makes his class. Let me up."

Heller pressed the buzzer.

In less than a minute Con was following her into the kitchen. He shot a glance at the paper open on the table. "You've seen it."

"So has a world of early risers. Think how diverted the morning commuters will be."

"It will pass."

"I hope my job doesn't."

He shrugged. "I'm sorry. I saw red when he kissed you."

"And purple and black. I like my job."

"I hate seeing you in scraps of clothing."

She burst out laughing. "Women wear less on the beach every day. I did when I was in Barbados."

"Yes, I know that. And I also am aware there are many nude beaches throughout the world where you could really be on display, but—"

"How many nude beaches have you visited?"

"A few, but that doesn't mean that I would want to see you cavort on one."

"But it would all right if some stacked blonde did just that for your personal pleasure. Right?"

Con glared at her. "Right, but that still doesn't mean that— "

"Double standard."

"Of course there's a double standard, Heller. I can like and admire the human body and still not want my wife on display."

"Well, I can like and admire the—*your* wife! I'm not your spouse in any way, shape, or form and—"

"What the hell do mean by that? Saying that you can like and admire. Were you going to say other men?"

"Of course. You look at women."

Con's face seemed to swell. "This is an archaic and out-of-date conversation. I have been an ardent feminist since college, well before the movement took fire, and I resent your—"

"And I resent your implication that I should not be looking at men when you feel free to scope out women."

"As I said, this is a dinosaur-age conversation."

"And you've been snookered."

"Someday I'm not going to be able to resist throttling you."

"You lay a hand on me, buster, and I'll punch your lights out."

Con saw the way her chin came up, the clenching and unclenching of her hands. His temper fled and he pulled her into his arms. "Forgive me. I didn't come here to fight with you." He rubbed his chin over her hair, loving the soft curls. "I still can't get used to this being cut so short." Lifting her chin, he pressed his mouth to hers. "Heller, will you forgive me?"

"Yes. I was being stupid."

"Yes." He chuckled when she pinched his waist.

"But you are beautiful when you're in a temper. If you hadn't been through such a traumatic experience lately, I would be tempted to stoke your fires more often."

"Really Con, I've recovered completely."

"I know you had a good checkup last week, but it's wise to pace yourself. That part in the musical is strenuous."

"And stimulating. I love it." She leaned back from him. "Have you been getting copies of my medical reports ever since the fire?"

He nodded. "Does that bother you?"

For a moment she was still, then she shook her head.

"Good. Then kiss me again."

Six

Nothing ever seemed settled between Con and Heller. At least that's the way it felt to Heller. There were moments when they fit like a matched set, yet there were times when they were poles apart, at loggerheads.

Two weeks after the play opened, Doodie decided to spend a few days with her fiancé, Leonard. He lived in a small town near Lake Erie, in the western part of the state. Heller and Doodie had thought the trip would be good for Simeon, and Father Densmore had been more than happy to bless the idea.

"The boy could use a few days vacation, and since he's bright enough to have his exams waived, that won't be a problem." The priest had grimaced at Heller. "Most of the public school systems don't give the children final examinations, but we find it gives them a sense of accomplishment. Take the boy, Doodie. It will be good for him." So Doodie had taken Simeon and Hector with her, leaving Heller alone in the apartment.

On Monday evening, the one night during the week that she didn't perform, she was going out to eat with Con. She saw him most evenings before she had to go onstage. Sometimes he even turned up at the theater when she was rehearsing. Several nights he had been waiting for her after the show and had taken her out for a late supper. She was always happy to see him, but still things didn't run smoothly for them all the time.

Just last night they'd had a flaming argument again because he thought Desi was too familiar with her.

Heller didn't examine her own feelings too closely, uneasily aware of how she had come to depend on Con, how life took on color when he was in it.

Con rang the downstairs bell, then opened the door when the buzzer sounded.

He was angry at himself. He'd had no intention of flying off the handle about Desi again last night, but seeing his flirtatious manner with Heller made his blood boil. Furthermore, the conversation he'd had with his sister earlier today still rankled him.

"You were once a most intrepid mountain climber," she'd said, appearing at his office door. "You fought in Vietnam and left relatively unscathed. You were a top rower and swimmer at Princeton. You've always had women by the score—"

"Get to the point, Ione."

"The point, dear brother, is that your personal life has always been smooth, and you were always in control. Now this one little lady, Heller Blane, has your world spinning off its axis."

"What do you mean?"

"I like this out-of-sync you. Being off balance has made you human, and I love it."

"Charming."

"Don't be surly. Once you marry her things will level out. Ta-ta for now. I have to get Will and remind him he's taking me out to dinner."

Long after Ione departed, Con had stared at the painting by Sargent on his wall. His sister was right. Heller had put him off keel and he didn't like the feeling.

Now, as the elevator doors opened, he stared at her, wondering what it was about her that had so totally captured him. "Hello."

"Hi."

She stepped into the elevator, and a wall of silence separated them all the way to the car.

"How does it feel to be in a play that has received great reviews?" Con asked as he headed north on Eighth Avenue.

"Good. Although that one reviewer, Dev Abrams, called it a clunker."

"But even he said that the stripper segment was well done."

"If I had a voice and if I ever took dance lessons, it would be 'appreciably better,' " she quoted.

"Dev Abrams is perhaps the toughest critic in this country, but he's highly respected, so you shouldn't feel damned by his faint praise. He made it sound as though your role contributed greatly to the show." Con laughed shortly. "Besides, Dev really isn't into musical comedy. Black tragedy is more his meat."

Heller twisted in her seat, straining the seat belt. "Do you know him?"

"Yes. We've been friends for many years. Dev, another man named Pacer Dillon, and I were at Princeton and in Vietnam together. The unholy three, that's us."

Heller felt a stab of envy that Dev Abrams and Pacer Dillon would know so much about Con, things that she longed to know. "Sounds like a close-knit group."

"Very."

He saw the anxious look in her eyes and read it accurately. He reached over and took her hand. "Don't fret. Being mentioned by Dev is good, you know, even when he isn't too complimentary."

She laughed. "He sounds like a veritable tyrant."

"In a way he is. He was a hell of a guy in every sport, a never-say-die type who dared anything. He was a flaming liberal, setting out to save the world. When he was accepted for law school, he decided he was going to write and later run for political office."

"What happened?"

"He married a free-lance photographer, then got a job as a correspondent for a news magazine. The two of them went to the Middle East, and they had a child there. Dev was happy, and was lauded as the incredible talent he is. Then his wife and little girl were kidnapped. Six months later he found their bodies. He came back to the United States bitter, angry, and hellbent on doing a little destruction of his own. He still writes and has published a few novels that have made him some good money, but doing theater reviews gives him the weapons he seems to need. He also dabbles in real estate and owns a sizable chunk of prime property right here in Manhattan."

"Wow! He sounds manic."

Con chuckled. "I don't think Dev would allow anything manic to take hold of him. He's the most tightly woven, self-contained individual I've ever known."

Heller shook her head. "He sounds like a paradox."

"He's that and more."

"And is Pacer Dillon the same?"

"No. He's quiet and unobtrusive, and I think he could be the most dangerous man alive. Pace is damned likable, very popular and easygoing, but I doubt few people really know him. He's tough as shoe leather, yet in Vietnam he took the time to found and support a home in Saigon for unwanted children."

"Another paradox."

"Yes."

"That makes three of you."

Con gave her an inscrutable look as he wheeled the car into a parking garage. He took his parking ticket from the attendant, then winced as the young man gunned the Ferrari's engine and careened away into the bowels of the garage.

"I thought we'd go to Joe Allen's tonight," he said as they walked out onto the street. "It's not very fancy, but it's always filled with theater people. We can do the see-and-be-seen scene."

Heller laughed. "That's fine with me."

"And . . . uh, also . . ."

He seemed hesitant, and she stared at him. "Yes?"

"Well, I hope you don't mind, but I was talking to Dev today, and he said he was having dinner here tonight. He asked us to join him for drinks."

"Dev Abrams?" She stopped and gaped at him. "We're having drinks with *Dev Abrams*, and you didn't warn me?"

"I know I should have, but I got caught up in a

meeting this afternoon and couldn't—" He looked at her closely. "What are you grinning about? I thought you were angry."

She shook her head and her grin broadened. "No. I just wanted you to grovel for a minute. I'm delighted to be meeting your friend."

"Good," said Con and held open the restaurant door for her. As he had said, Joe Allen's was rather plain, but even on a Monday night there were quite a few Broadway luminaries there. Con asked the maître d' for Mr. Abrams's table, and they were led to one in a corner.

Three people were sitting at the table, a man and two women. The black-haired black-eyed man, who looked as though his name should be Lucifer, was gazing insolently at both the blonde on his right and then at the redhead on his left. When he saw he was to be interrupted, he frowned.

"Never mind the dark looks, Dev," Con drawled. "Save it for those who are impressed by you."

Dev Abrams's entire face lightened as he grinned with joy. He stood so abruptly, he set the table rocking. "About time you showed up, Rad." He vigorously shook Conrad's hand. "I thought you weren't coming. Come on, sit down. Elaine, Jan, move closer. Give them room."

Once they were all seated, Dev's black eyes fixed on Heller. "I know your lovely companion. But how I know her. What a beauty!"

"Don't speak of me as though I'm a mannequin. I don't like it," Heller said tartly.

"Whew, feel the flames." Dev glanced at Con. "Rad, you're smitten."

Con felt a heat in his face, but it wasn't embarrassment. Dev had always been able to penetrate the extraneous. "Right as usual. May I present my fiancée, Heller Blane?" He smiled benignly at Heller when she glared at him.

"Do I take it that this engagement is news to your fiancée?"

"Only old news," Heller said. Then she shrank down in her seat when Con chuckled and kissed the nape of her neck.

"Why don't you cancel your table and eat with us, Rad?"

"No, I think we'll stick with just drinks. How's that?"

"If that's it, I'll take it." Dev leaned across the woman named Elaine and picked up Heller's left hand. "No ring yet. Rad didn't used to be so slow."

Heller pulled back her hand, an unwilling smile touching her mouth at the man's outrageousness. "I don't need a ring."

"But she's getting one." Con curved his hand around her neck when he felt her stiffen.

"Your voice is not operatic and you are no Pavlova, Heller Blane, but you torched that stage the other evening," Dev said seriously.

Heller was taken aback by his words. "Thank you."

"You're welcome. You will," he went on, his voice becoming a trifle arrogant, "make money with your fire, even if your techniques are rusty."

"Thank you, O mighty sultan." She bowed her head in mock obeisance.

For a moment there was a flash of surprise on Dev's face, then he looked at a laughing Con. "You didn't tell me she was so savvy."

"Very savvy and very brave." Con took her hand and lifted it to his lips. "She has me in knots."

"I can see you're really upset by it." Dev flashed a twisted smile.

To be with Dev was to waltz with wildfire, Heller thought. She wasn't sure if that made her happy or sad, but it certainly wasn't dull.

Heller was sorry when they left the threesome and went to their own table. "He's a very complex man."

"Yes."

"There's pain . . . and anger in his eyes."

"If you'd known his wife, you would understand. She was a great woman and bright as hell. They were on fire for each other."

"But who is it that he can't forgive?"

"Himself," Con whispered. "He'd gone on a short assignment out of Beirut when Felicity and Esther were taken. He was drunk for a month after finding out they'd been killed and he kept muttering that he should have been there." Con sighed. "Pacer and I couldn't seem to reach him. It was hell. When we were at Princeton, we were mavericks, misfits. We didn't seem to belong anyplace, but we went everywhere and anywhere and did what we chose. But when Felicity died, a part of Dev died with her . . . and we couldn't do anything about it."

"Tell me more about Pacer," Heller said.

Con smiled. "He's an incredible man. He didn't come back from Nam with Dev and me. He stayed on for several years. They say he married, but I don't know for sure and I don't ask. He calls me once in a while. He has an uncanny sense of danger where Dev and I are concerned. Perhaps it's because he's part Sioux that he's rather mystical." Con shrugged as though his coat had suddenly become too tight.

"I understand," she said.

He looked at her steadily for a minute. "I think you do." '

"Is Pacer in the U.S.?"

"I think he is. He didn't say when we last spoke, but I had the feeling he was in this area."

"You have unusual friends."

Con studied her for several seconds. "Yes, I do. But they're good, loyal friends, and we all take care of one another. If I were ever in danger, Dev and Pacer would be there in an instant to help me." He took her hands in his. "And since you're my lady, they'd do the same for you."

Her mouth trembling, Heller forced herself to meet his gaze. "You know . . . about . . ."

"Only part. Will you tell me the whole story?"

"I don't want you involved," she whispered.

His hands tightened on hers. "I'm already involved, Heller. I'm in your life to stay. Talk to me."

She pulled her hands free and folded them in her lap. Without looking at him, she began. "My mother was a wonderful woman. As I told you, she had her own small accounting business. She was thrilled when one of the bigger construction companies in Syracuse, where she lived, hired her. The company was run by two brothers, Anthony and Bruno Domini, and was called the Domini Brothers.

It was a coup for my mother to get them as clients. But she was truly a wonder with figures."

Heller paused and took a deep breath, pressing the tips of her fingers against her forehead. "She discovered discrepancies in their books and called them on it. They threatened her, but she figured that she could go to jail if she didn't do something, so she turned them in to the authorities. Shortly after that, a building they'd constructed collapsed, so her testimony about undercutting and falsifying records became crucial."

The painful memories contorted her features as she looked up at Con. "I was at the university. I didn't know anything until Mother's lawyer called and told me I should come home to support her during the trial. He was as shocked as I was when I told him I hadn't known the story. I took a leave of absence from school and returned home."

Heller paused again, gratefully sipping her lemon-flavored tonic water. "When it was over, the two brothers were convicted, along with some of their workers." She stared at Con. "Two people had been killed when one of the Domini buildings collapsed. They threatened Mother. Once our car blew up. Another time we found our dog poisoned . . ." Heller hauled in a shuddering breath. "So we were put into the witness protection program. Our names were changed, even our social security numbers. We had to leave everything behind, never contact our friends again.

"We were relocated here, to New York City. Mother got a job with an accounting firm and I started taking classes at NYU. Then, not too long before I met you, Mother had a heart attack, and—" She pressed her hand to her mouth to stifle a sob.

"Darling, don't." Con moved closer so he could embrace her. "I get the picture. You don't need to tell me any more."

"Now that I've started, I want to tell it all."

"All right."

"The doctor said that Mother needed bypass surgery. But we didn't have the money. I interviewed for dozens of jobs, but without a college degree or any secretarial skills, the best I could do was cocktail waitress at the Andre."

"And you worked two shifts."

"Yes. I was desperate for money."

"That's why I put the ten thousand dollars into your purse."

"I was both grateful and angry. I didn't want you to think I was a—"

"I thought you beautiful and warm and the woman I wanted to marry."

"Con . . ."

She caressed his cheek. He grasped her wrist, moved her hand to his mouth, and warmly kissed her palm. Her hand was trembling.

"I'm going to order something to eat," he said.

"I'm not very hungry."

"Some bouillabaisse and some fruit, then we'll go." He stared directly into her eyes. "I'm staying with you tonight." He pressed one finger lightly to her lips when she would have spoken. "Don't argue. Just talking about this has been traumatic for you, and I don't like the idea of your being alone in that apartment tonight."

He was right, Heller thought. She was feeling on edge, simply from remembering that terrible time, and the warehouse could seem quite threatening at night.

"All right," she said, and was rewarded with a brilliant smile.

"Good," he said. "Now let's order."

"Well, here we are," Heller said nervously as the elevator doors opened onto the apartment. She flicked a switch to turn on the light in the entryway. "Can I get you something to drink?"

Con grabbed her arm as she started walking away,

spinning her around to face him. "No, thank you," he said politely, then gave her a little shake. "Calm down, Heller. You've been as jumpy as a cat at a dog show. I'm not going to attack you."

Her shoulders slumped as she sighed with exhaustion. "I know. It's just been—"

"A long evening." He put his arms around her. "Come on. You should go directly to bed."

Together they crossed the living room and walked down a hall to her bedroom. Con stopped at the door.

"You get ready for bed," he said, "and I'll warm up some milk for you."

She turned abruptly, and he was pleased to see a flash of temper in her eyes. "Warm milk?" she repeated. "Forget it. The mere thought is revolting."

"It's good for you," he said. With his hands on her shoulders he turned her back around and gave her a gentle shove into her bedroom. "If you're not ready for bed by the time I get back, I'll be obliged to help you."

She tossed him a scathing look, then slammed the door in his face. He chuckled as he walked back down the hall to the kitchen.

When he returned with a mug of warm milk, she was in bed, but her expression was mutinous.

"Good girl," he said. "Now drink all your milk or you won't get a good-night kiss."

She wrinkled her nose as he handed her the mug. After a tentative sip of the milk she looked up at him. "Where were you thinking of sleeping?" she asked almost shyly.

"In Simeon's room. You don't think he'd mind, do you?"

She shook her head. "You could sleep here," she said after a pause.

He gazed at her wide bed and was almost unbearably tempted to strip off his clothes and leap in beside her. But then he took a step back and shook his head.

"No, Heller. If I got into bed with you now, it wouldn't be to sleep." Her eyes widened. She seemed about to speak, but he held up a hand to stop her. "I don't think you're ready for that yet. I know your body has recovered from its injuries, but your emotions need more time to heal."

He leaned over and gave her a chaste kiss on the forehead. "Good night, Heller."

Heller finished every last drop of the warm milk, but with Con in another bed only a few feet away from her, it didn't help her sleep.

The next afternoon Con was wondering where to take Heller for dinner after the show that night, when John buzzed him on the intercom.

"Yes?"

"Phone call for you," John said. "It's Pacer Dillon."

Pacer, Con thought. Somehow he didn't believe it was mere coincidence that his old friend was turning up now. He picked up the phone.

"Hey, Pacer. Funny you should call. I was just talking about you last night. . . . What? When? You're kidding. Early parole because of good behavior? . . . How did you find out? . . . I'll take her to the theater this evening and pick her up when the show's over. Have you talked to Dev? . . . He might be at the paper. . . . I'm sure Heller wants to meet you too. Thanks, Pacer. I'll see you later."

He hung up and drummed his fingers on the desk as he stared at the phone. He had to make sure Heller was protected without alarming and frightening her. Quickly, he dialed her number. She wasn't home, but he left a message on her machine that he would pick her up at seven to take her to the theater and that he was treating her to a home-cooked dinner at his apartment after the show.

"Can you really cook?" Heller asked skeptically as Con drove through Manhattan, heading for his apartment in the East Eighties. She had been shocked when she'd returned from rehearsal to find his message on her answering machine. Shocked and excited. She was going to Con's apartment for dinner . . . maybe for the night. Regardless of what he'd said last night, she did feel emotionally ready to make love with him again. She loved him.

"Of course I can cook," he said. "Wait until you see what I've got waiting for you." He grinned suggestively, and she laughed. Heller found that driving through Manhattan at night had a mesmerizing effect. The city had a luster all its own. The weather was cool, the sky clear. Its blackness was set off by the hundreds of lights on the streets and in the buildings. She leaned back and watched the city night unfold for her. But as they turned into the underground garage of Con's apartment building, she saw that he was watching his rearview mirror intently. "What is it?"

"Nothing, I'm sure. I just didn't recognize the car that followed us down here." He parked in his reserved spot. "Wait. I'll come around and get your door."

Heller had no intention of waiting in the car if Con could be in jeopardy. Looking around the car, she spotted a tool kit behind the driver's seat. she removed a small wrench from it. It was better than nothing.

Con was standing beside the car, checking out the massive garage. She quietly opened her door and slipped out, crouching low. She would back in at once if Conrad said it was all clear.

"Where's the girl?"

The sudden rough voice frightened her, and she tightened her fist around the wrench.

"Get out of here," Con said. "This is a private garage and well patrolled."

"Answer the question . . . Mr. Wendel."

Heller edged upward. Three men were standing at the back of the car, facing Con. Three of them! Did they have guns? Where was security?

"Where is Heller Blane?" the rough voice asked.

"Not here."

"That's a lie. We saw a woman in the car with you, Wendel."

Without warning the men leapt as one at Con.

Heller jumped to her feet and tore around the car. She hooked her arm around the neck of the nearest man and hauled back. He cursed angrily as he fought to loosen her arm. Then, with a jerk of his burly body, he flung her off him. She fell to the cement floor but rolled quickly to her feet in a lithe movement.

"I've got her," the man shouted. "She's here."

He moved forward to grab her. As his enormous hands reached for her, she kicked upward with all her strength, past his body to his chin. The force of her kick threw her off balance and she fell against a parked car, winded.

The man stumbled back against a support stanchion with a resounding crack. He didn't fall, though. He shook himself like a wet bear and glared at her. "Bitch! See if I don't break your neck for this."

She barely noticed the sound of squealing tires and a racing engine, then a man called out, "We're here, Rad!" The confident voice echoed in the cement chamber, bouncing off the walls.

Two men burst from a car and threw themselves upon the attackers. Her breath tight in her chest, Heller watched as Con finished off his man with a hard right to the jaw.

"Con!" she called, but her voice was a mere whistle of sound. Still, he heard her.

"Heller! Are you all right? Dammit, I told you to stay in the car." In two strides he was beside her, enfolding her in his arms.

The other two men quickly dispatched their adversaries, then grinned at each other.

"You barely had to lift your pinkie, Pace," Dev said. "The little lady had already taken the fight out of him."

"And yours was much smaller, twit."

"Thanks, both of you," Con said. "We'd better call the police."

"No cops," Dev said. "We'll take them with us and ask them some elementary questions. Nothing that will tax their hat-size IQs."

"Take it easy, Dev, I mean it."

"I promise the slime will live, Rad, but we'll know by morning what we're dealing with. Won't we, Pace?"

"Yes." The other man stepped into the light. He was taller than Con or Dev, his sun-streaked blond hair looking almost white in the harsh lights. His face was rough-hewn, craggy, as though an amateur sculptor had shaped it, crooking the nose, coarsely chiseling the jaw and cheekbones. "Hello, beautiful lady. I'm your protector, Pacer Creekwood Dillon, from points east and west." He swept Heller a bow.

"How do you do, Mr. Dillon."

"Pacer, ma'am."

"Thank you for what you've done, Pacer."

"You're most welcome. You done good, old buddy. She's a rare one, indeed."

"So, Heller," Con said, "now you've met all the sins of my past."

"Not all, I'm sure," she said dryly.

"She's spunky as hell too," Dev said, grinning at Heller. Then his smile faded and he turned to Con. "This should be the end of it, Rad, but we'll double-check. You take care of your lady. Good night."

"Good night, beautiful lady," Pacer said. "We'll take care of this mess. Incidentally, you have a great kick. Only a dancer would know how to throw a punch with her foot that way. Mighty nice."

The two men loaded the assailants into a car, then with a final wave drove off.

Con turned to Heller. "Don't you ever endanger yourself like that again."

"Con, there were three of them. Even you can't handle that, Superman."

"I saw that kick of yours. It was a beauty and would have taken out anyone but that mule." He hauled her against his chest. "I was so scared when I heard one of them say he'd gotten you. Heller, I'm not letting you out of my sight."

"I thought they would kill you." She gulped in a breath, trying to stem the sobs that were rising in her throat. Her arms curled around his neck and she clung tightly.

"Nothing is going to part us again," he said in a husky voice. "I thought you knew that."

"They were nasty and the three of them were on you."

"I love you, you spunky, outspoken lady."

Heller felt as though she'd been blown apart and then magically fitted back together again. She was entirely new because he'd said that.

Hips bumping gently, they walked to the elevator. Con inserted a key into the panel.

"Is that just for your apartment?" she asked.

He nodded. "I have the top floor."

The elevator opened into a large, circular two-story foyer. The marble tiles of swirled cream and peach on the floor matched the French cloth wallpaper. Beyond the foyer was an elegantly furnished living room, and a stairway curved up the far wall to the second floor.

Conrad watched her closely as they walked through the living room. Her interest in his apartment seemed to be overcoming any aftershock. He was disconcerted, though, when he saw amusement on her face as they entered the two-story library.

"What's so funny, Heller?" He had had the room designed to his own specifications, with mahogany shelves lining the walls, all filled with books. When she laughed out loud it both irritated and titillated him.

"Do you sit here at night and play your violin, Mr. Holmes?"

His gaze roved the room and his mouth twitched with amusement. "So it looks like Sherlock's den, does it?"

"A tad."

"Brat."

She took his hand. "I'm being witchy. I'm sorry."

"You're being wonderful . . . and very brave." He lifted her hand to his mouth and playfully licked her fingers. "You have kept me on my toes since our first meeting. I can see our marriage will be an exciting one."

"Con—"

"Indulge me this once. Let's go upstairs." Keeping her hand in his, he backed out and strolled over to the circular stairway.

"You don't really have to show me your whole apartment," she said, holding back.

He smiled down at her, seeing the slash of color in her cheeks, the sudden shy look. "Let me show you my lair. It's all done in wolf and tiger pelts."

"How fitting," she said tartly.

He gestured that she precede him, and the sight of her long legs and slender body sent his libido into warp speed. "You do have the power," he whispered.

On the second floor he opened a door and led her into a massive sitting room decorated in cream and wedgwood blue. "You also have the greatest legs, Heller, and I love your hips and backside."

"Stop that." She turned to face him, and her hair and eyes echoed the jewel tones in the Persian carpet.

"Stop what? Looking at you? Never. It's my favorite thing to do. Well, almost my favorite."

She should have given him a verbal blistering that would have scorched his eyebrows. When she felt the mirth rise in her again, she fought it, but it came out in a gasp and a smile anyway. "You are the most outrageous person I've ever known."

"I'll do better." It pleased him more than anything had in a long time to hear her chuckle. He sensed what it had taken for her to tamp down her fear when the three men had accosted him. She was a pearl in his life, and he was going to keep her safe.

Placing his arm across her shoulders, he guided her to a door in the opposite wall. "This is my bedroom."

The room was mammoth, with the huge bed holding center stage.

"It's very nice." She had the sensation of standing on one foot, off balance, teetering.

"Look around while I change my clothes. Sit in the library or relax in the sitting room. I won't be long."

He disappeared into a closet that seemed to be a room in itself. For a minute she wandered around the room, finally approaching the bed.

On impulse she sat down on it. It was firm and comfortable.

"You look wonderful there," Con said from behind her.

She turned and stared into his eyes. He slid across the width of the bed, coming to rest beside her. "It's very firm," she said.

"Yes," he said indifferently.

"It must have been difficult getting it up here to this apartment."

"I suppose. Heller, do you know how long I've dreamed of having you with me again?"

"Less than a year."

He touched her cheek. "As long as I've known you."

"That's what I said." She coughed to clear her throat.

"You did that the first time we made love, darling."

"What?" Heller knew she should stand. Con wasn't holding her. There was no reason to stay seated on the bed. But his eyes chained her.

"Your voice squeaked like that."

"Genetic flaw."

"I love it. I hope our girls have it."

"Con . . . enough, be sensible, don't talk commitment." She couldn't stem the floodtide of hope that rose in her. Darn him for making her want him so.

"How about talking love?" He leaned forward so their lips were touching.

The feathery, ticklish sensation had her blood bubbling through her veins. Heat was rushing through her. Con's touch had done the same thing ever since they'd first made love.

With slow tender pressure his lips parted hers. "Touch me, darling," he murmured into her mouth.

As though she had been poised for this moment, she let her hands eagerly explore him, examine him, caress him as though he were precious porcelain. When he groaned she became bolder. She leaned closer to him and bit him gently on the neck. Her fingers quickly undid the buttons on his shirt.

Slowly, breathlessly, they peeled the clothes from each other's body.

When Con fell back on the bed, Heller was on top of him. Her mouth found his nipples, and she kissed and nipped them as he had once done to hers.

"Enough," he said. His voice was rough with passion. He twisted her under him and began his own love search, as though he could caress every pore on her body. Her hipbones were laved by his tongue, each toe on her feet was savored.

She felt a melting begin from within. Her body became liquid, her skin slipped away. Her being joined with his so easily.

When his tongue touched her in the most intimate way, her body jerked and arched with the ever-rising passion that was controlling both of them.

"Con!" She pulled at his shoulders until he slid up her body.

"I'm with you all the way, darling."

With a gentle thrust he took her and together they scaled the Olympic heights of ecstasy, casting themselves beyond the earth to the stars. Love exploded within her.

Seven

For the next two weeks, Con spent more time at the warehouse apartment than he did at his own place. Heller sometimes wasn't sure if it was because he couldn't bear to be apart from her or because he was still worried about her safety.

He'd finally admitted that he'd known there was a threat of danger the night they'd been attacked. Pacer had called him at his office with the news that Bruno and Anthony Domini were out on parole and were headed for New York City. Pacer couldn't figure out how they'd picked up Heller's trail, though. He had a suspicion someone had tipped them off.

As for herself, Heller had mixed feelings about Con's constant presence. She loved him, and sometimes felt like shouting the news to the world. Other times, though, he seemed to suffocate her. His personality was so strong, so overwhelming at times, she wondered if she was making any of the decisions about her life anymore. Con wanted to marry her, and often that seemed to her the most wonderful thing that could happen. But she didn't feel she had control of her own life yet, and didn't want to rush into anything.

The apartment quickly became crowded, because a week after Con and Haller became lovers again, Doodie's fiancé arrived. He'd finally gotten a job in Manhattan, although it wouldn't start for a month. He and Doodie were planning on marrying shortly thereafter.

Simeon, who'd begun laughing all the time and even used a few words, almost retreated into silence again when Leonard moved in. But the gentle, bespectacled man with the wide smile quickly won him over.

"I think if you weren't planning on adopting him, we would," Leonard told Heller one day as they watched Doodie help the boy with a painting. "I hope you know we're going to be very interested and close godparents."

Heller kissed Leonard on the cheek and smiled.

"And thanks for saying we could take Simeon camping, Heller. Two weeks in the Adirondacks will be so good for him."

"I know, Len. He loves both of you."

"I think he'll want to take Hector with us. Is that a problem?"

She chuckled. "Try parting those two. Hector is now Simeon's dog."

"That's what Doodie says. A dog is a good companion on a camping trip, so we'll take him."

"Fine. Hector will be ecstatic."

Leonard laughed.

That afternoon Heller took Simeon for their usual walk, Hector gamboling around them. There was a small park near the river and it had become their exercise and special time together.

"I love you, Simeon." She smoothed her hand through his tightly curled black hair.

"I love you, Heller."

"Oh, God, oh, God, Simeon. You do pick your times." She cried, holding him close. "That is your very first complete sentence to me and the words were so beautiful." When she felt his thin arms around her, she sighed. "I'll miss you when you go to the mountains with Doodie and Leonard, but you'll have a good time."

He smiled up at her and nodded.

She dried her eyes. "Come on, pal, it's time to go back. I have to get to work."

"Leonard and I are cooking tonight."

"And are you going to talk to Doodie and him too?"

"Yes, and to Con."

At rehearsal the next day Heller was surprised to see Desi there. Usually the assistant director ran the rehearsal.

"Hey, Heller!" he called to her when she was through with her number. "Would you come here a minute? I want to talk to you."

"All right, Desi. Let me get some juice first." With a towel around her neck and a glass of orange juice in her hand, she walked back to Desi, who was seated in the fifth row of the orchestra.

"Would you mind reading this?" He handed her a bound sheaf of papers.

Puzzled, she glanced at the top page and read: *Ablaze*. A movie. "All right," she said. She walked back a few rows, made herself comfortable in an aisle seat, and began reading.

Long after rehearsal was over she was still turning pages rapidly. At last she finished the script and sighed.

"That was just a rough draft," Desi said, walking up the aisle toward her, "but what do you think, Heller? What's more important, do you mind?"

She lifted her head and stared at him. "It's very good and very exciting. You've made it into a love story, but the part about my rescuing those two children from the fire is accurate. Almost too accurate." She dabbed at the beads of sweat on her upper lip. It had been more painful than she'd imagined it could be to go over the moments when she'd been in the fire.

"Would you be interested in being a consultant on the piece for me? It's going to be a TV movie and it will be shot in Barbados. I'm leaving in a week to scout out possible settings and shoot some of the action shots that require stunt people. It'll be for about three weeks. I want to make sure everything is authentic. We could have the understudy to do your part here. What do you say?"

Barbados! she thought. That beautiful island that she'd loved so much. Would this be the opportunity to get her life in order, to come to grips with the Domini brothers, with Con? Simeon would be away camping with Leonard and Doodie anyhow. And as for Con, she needed time to try to look objectively at their relationship . . . if that was possible. It certainly wasn't when they were together. When she was with him she was all up in the air, out of control.

"Heller, why are you frowning? What are you thinking? You haven't answered my question."

"What? Oh, sorry, Desi. I think it would be great to go to Barbados and work on this, but I've never done this sort of thing."

"You were there, Heller, you are *Ablaze*."

"The male lead in the play. He seems familiar."

"He should. I patterned him after Wendel. Anyone who isn't totally blind can see he's hung up on you."

"But—"

"And if you weren't so hung up on him, I would make a run at you myself."

"I'm not hung up," she protested. Did the whole world see that she loved Con? "You're a friend, Desi, and I appreciate that, but I don't know about this."

"Why don't you think about it?"

"All right."

"What do you think tall, dark, and rich will have to say if you go?"

"I really don't know."

Heller decided the next day to go to Barbados, but she had trouble finding the right time to tell Con. Though she saw him every day, when they were apart she often thought of what she wanted to say to him. Then, when she was with him, words fled, feelings erupted.

The afternoon that Doodie, Leonard, Simeon, and Hector left for the camping trip, Con was at the apartment.

"What will you do now that Simeon's going camping?" he asked her as they watched the van pull away. Simeon's face was pressed to the window, his white teeth gleaming in a wobbly but happy smile.

Heller stiffened though she continued waving. "What do you mean?"

"You've been hiding something from me, Heller. What is it?"

"You could get in trouble climbing into people's brains," she said tartly. Unbidden tears filled her eyes. "I'm going to miss Simeon so much."

"Darling!" Con gathered her into his arms, well aware that she hadn't answered his question. "It's only two weeks. He'll be back in no time, full of sunshine and tall tales. We won't be able to sleep at night for listening to all the great things he's seen."

She laughed, swallowing a sob. "True. He's a wonderful boy. I'm so happy to be adopting him."

"Good." They turned to reenter the warehouse. "Now tell me what's bothering you."

Heller inhaled a shaky breath. "I'm going to accompany Desi to Barbados for a few weeks to be a consultant on a movie he's shooting. It's called *Ablaze* and it's partly about my experiences in the fire."

Con's arm tightened around her waist.

"When was all this decided?"

"A couple of days ago," she said evasively.

"Would you have told me of your plans if I hadn't pressed you?"

His eyes were molten emerald, his anger sparking off him like an electric charge. "Of course I would have. Con, I'm just doing him a favor."

"You know damn well I don't like the way he is with you."

"Well, that's too damned bad." She stormed off toward the elevator. "This is strictly a job. I will be paid for doing it. I leave tomorrow and I will be back in three weeks." She turned back and faced him defiantly.

"Excuse me. I think I'll go to the office." He stalked away from her, his back stiff.

"Do that." Heller bit her lip to keep from calling him back.

That evening she expected to eat alone the meager meal she always consumed before going to the theater.

When Con arrived at six and began helping her wash the vegetables for her salad, she couldn't find the words to tell him how glad she was to see him. The urge to drop to her knees and beg him to love her forever was overwhelming. Instead, she carefully, methodically, tore up some lettuce. Silently, they sat down to eat, but Heller barely picked at her food.

"Aren't you hungry?" he asked.

"Yes . . . no. I've discovered my stomach isn't up for food before curtain. I seem to be eating more in the middle of the day." She glanced at him, then away.

He eyed her over his wine glass. "I think you have filled out a little, but your appetite isn't what it should be."

She swallowed. "Con . . . about this trip—"

"Forget it, Heller. Sometimes our conversations get out of hand. I don't think we agree about Carleton Desmond."

"I suppose you're right," she answered tightly.

He carried his plate to the sink, rinsed it, and put it into the dishwasher. She had been shocked at first when Con had helped around the apartment. Now she was somewhat used to it.

"I should be going soon," she said, rising to clear away her own dishes.

"I'll drive you. I have a hankering to see the show once more."

"But you must have seen it half a dozen times."

"Keeping track of my investment." The acid in his smile touched her like hot needles.

"You must be pleased that it's a hit."

"Of course."

They were like combatants in an arena, she thought, and turned away.

He hooked an arm around her waist, drawing her back to him. "I hate it when we argue."

She locked her hands behind his head. "So do I." She kissed him deeply, her mouth open to his, tongue touching tongue.

At last Con dragged his mouth from hers. "Come on. If I don't take you to the theater now, I'll take you to bed."

She pressed an index finger against his warm lips. "I think I'd like that."

Con breathed in her essence, loving the elusive fresh scent that was hers alone. "Lady, don't push your luck."

While driving to the theater, Con held her hand. "Three weeks is a long time. I'll miss you."

"I'll miss you too."

"Knock 'em dead tonight."

"I'll try."

"My parents would like us to go out to their place for dinner some evening, perhaps when you get back."

"I'd like that."

"All right, I'll set a time."

He parked in a space near the stage entrance.

"Why do you do that?" she asked as he opened the door for her. "You'll get a ticket."

"Let's not worry about that."

"I'm law-abiding."

"You're also prickly as hell." He walked her to the dressing room she shared with some of the other actors and dancers. "I'll pick you up here."

She closed the door in his face and leaned against it. Those laser eyes of his could peel the skin off a grape without touching the flesh. He was being civil as hell, but he was like a bomb about to explode. Con was a barbarian in Savile Row suits.

Con smiled at the policeman who was walking around his car. "I'm going to move it, Officer."

'Thank you, sir. Have a good evening."

"You have one as well," Con said absently. Damn Desmond for taking her away, he thought. It was a crucial time in their relationship. He had sensed since the confrontation with the thugs in his underground garage that she was not entirely convinced they could have a life together. He needed time to convince her of the rightness of their future, not a three-week separation.

Heller's performance that night was stellar. There was a recklessness, a hot intensity about it that had the audience applauding long and hard when she was through.

"Dammit," Con muttered under his breath. "If she gets any better, she'll be offered starring roles."

When he went backstage after the finale, he could barely get into her dressing room.

"What did you think of our girl tonight, Wendel?"

"She was great, Desi. I'm sure you didn't need me to tell you that."

"No, I didn't, as a matter of fact. Heller has a great future in the theater."

Con saw Desi's smile as malicious. "Does she? Won't that be up to her?"

"It won't be up to anyone else."

Con stared at the other man. Anger at the impending separation from Heller had his hands clenching into fists. He would have liked to punch the dapper director in the mouth. Instead, he turned to Heller.

"Hurry, darling," he said. "I want as much time alone with you tonight as possible." When she was ready, he took her arm and hustled her out of the theater.

"I'm going to make you supper at home," he said. "You threw everything into that part tonight. I'll bet ten men go home and divorce their wives because of you."

She laughed tiredly as he handed her into the Ferrari. "You haven't gotten a ticket yet?"

"The policeman and I are old friends."

"Lawbreaker." She couldn't smother the yawn that rose in her throat.

"Close your eyes. When we get home, you can take a shower and I'll make you an omelet."

"I think I'll just take the shower and go to bed."

"You have to eat something." Glancing at her, Con realized he was talking to himself. She had fallen asleep, her head slipping sideways. He eased his arm around her and pulled her close, making a pillow of his shoulder for her.

After parking near the warehouse, Con lifted her from her seat. Taken aback at her fragility, he was certain that whatever weight she'd gained in the past month, she'd lost some of it in the performance she'd put on that evening.

Cradling her easily in his arms, he was able to unlock the door and carry her to the elevator.

When he was laying her on her bed her eyes fluttered open.

"Wh-where am I? Oh, dear, I must have fallen asleep."

"You're exhausted from working too hard."

"No, not really. Sometimes I do get caught up in the play and feel like a rag doll at the end."

"And sometimes you forget that you should be getting more rest. You were badly traumatized by that fire."

"Con, that was ages ago. The doctors told me I'm fine—"

"And that you should get plenty of rest." He leaned over her, and she reached up to kiss him.

"You have the softest lips but the toughest mouth," she whispered. "You're a paradox, Conrad Wendel." Her fingers feathered over his face. "Your jaw line is forged iron, but you have a dimple that appears every now and then."

"May I explore you as well?"

"I suppose it's only fair."

Her voice was barely audible but he still heard her, and his libido climbed into the danger zone. He lowered his head and touched his tongue to the cleavage showing at her blouse closing. "You have wonderful breasts."

"Too small."

"Perfect. They could feed me." He stared at her. "Would you nurse me, Heller? It would be a lifetime job."

"What's the pay? Are there good benefits? Vacation time? My father taught me to ask those questions." Did her hoarse voice tell Con how fluttery she felt at his nearness, at the thought of spending her life with him?

"Smart man. The benefits are excellent, including dental care, sick leave, and maternity leave. Your trips would be paid for by the company . . . me. How does traveling to Europe sound for starters?"

"Sleeping in hostels?"

"I was thinking more along the lines of cruising the Mediterranean in a yacht with a kingsize bed." He nibbled her shoulder, his teeth nipping at her tender flesh. "Incredibly sexy."

"You're crazy." Heller gripped his head, pulling him toward her.

The sexy huskiness in her voice drove him wild. It took all his strength to keep his rising passion under control.

"Con, you're trembling."

"You do that to me, Heller."

"You have a fiery effect on me too." She pulled him tight to her, burying her face into his neck.

"Did you sob just then, darling?"

"No, no. Don't pull back. I'm just being foolish. It's . . . it's so potent between us."

"Yes, as it's always been since the first time."

"Where are you going?"

"Nowhere. I just have to love you a little more."

"But you're ready, I can sense it."

He grinned. "Darling, I'm always ready around you."

"You look like a little boy with your hair tousled that way."

"I feel like a little boy on Christmas morning." He slid down her body and unbuttoned her blouse. He coaxed her nipples to pebble hardness, then took one breast into his mouth, sucking as though all the world's sustenance came from her. "Umm, Heller mine, you are luscious."

Slipping down farther, he let his tongue stab at her navel until her body began its own rhythmic response.

"Con!"

"Not yet, love, soon." He moved still lower, gently parting her legs before he began caressing her inner thigh. With one hot lunge his tongue intruded intimately, taking her in the same elemental way that a man will always claim the woman he loves.

Her hands spasmodically clutched his hair as the rising tide of passion threatened to overwhelm her.

Con couldn't contain his own powerful need. He covered her body with his and entered her gently but forcefully, taking her in one strong, smooth stroke.

"Con!"

"I'm with you, Heller." He felt on fire. His nerve endings stung and tingled, his body trembled with anticipation of the impending explosion as he began the rhythm of the ages.

They crested together, clinging, touching, on fire for each other.

"Heller, don't let me go. Keep me."

"Oh, Con, it was so wonderful."

When he saw her fight a yawn, he chuckled. "I have a feeling an omelet is out."

"Could I have it for breakfast?"

"Yes, ma'am," he whispered to her, cuddling her close to him, having no intention of leaving her.

The next morning Heller woke and tried to stretch, but she was chained to something. Chained? Opening her eyes, she oriented herself at once. Con was still holding her. Turning her head slowly so that she could look at him, she inhaled deeply. His mouth was inches from hers, slightly open. She ached to touch that wonderful face, to kiss those lips, but she was loath to disturb him.

How wild they'd been with each other last night.

Without Con life would be a private hell. One thing was for sure, she had no intention of turning him down again if he ever formally proposed to her. Even if she had to experience the pain of losing him sometime in the future, she was determined to grasp and embrace the present. To hell with what happened down the road.

A thrill went through her as she pressed her palm to her abdomen. Someday Con's child might rest there.

"Darling? What is it? Are you in pain? Was I too rough with you last night? Tell me."

"So many questions." She laughed. "I'm fine. I was just relaxing."

"Are you sure? You're very delicate and—"

"Like a prize mare I'm delicate! Will you stop that? I'm just fine."

"And I'm going to see that you stay that way."

"I have to get up." She paused, not wanting to mention their parting.

"Right. You have a flight to Barbados in the early afternoon. I'll get the omelet started, but first I want my kiss."

She cupped his face in her hands and feathered her lips over his, then kissed him passionately.

"Dammit, Heller. The hell with the omelet."

"No, no, I have to get ready."

She was smiling but there was a sheen of tears in her eyes. Con felt a jolt of pain, as though someone were digging at him with a dull knife. "Darling? Are you sure you're all right?"

"Quite sure." She kissed his nose. "But I am hungry. Let's fix breakfast together."

Con felt her gaze on him all the while they ate the fluffy omelet and dry toast they'd prepared.

By the time they were dressed, his nerves felt electrified. It was as though he'd already entered the emptiness that he'd lived in when she'd disappeared after they'd first made love.

Before he left, he kissed her with all the love inside him. "Will you call me every night?"

"Yes."

"I'll miss you, Heller."

She hugged him tightly. "I'll miss you too."

He forced himself to step away from her and walk toward the elevator. "Call me," he said over his shoulder.

"I will."

The sadness and something in her expression he could call only fear alarmed him. As soon as he reached his office, he made a call to an unlisted number. "Pace? I might have a problem. I think Heller's still frightened of the Domini brothers. Check it out, will you? Thanks. I appreciate it."

Heller couldn't concentrate on what Desi was saying as they sat at the gate waiting to board their plane. "What? Oh, yes, I have everything in order, I even brought the journal I started in the hospital to keep myself from going crazy with boredom."

"Good. Now, will you relax?"

"Don't worry about me, Desi, I'll be fine." Heller knew she'd been too abrupt, but a hollow feeling assailed her at leaving Con.

Their row was called, and as Heller stood up she

bumped into someone. She started to apologize, then gasped. "Mr. Domini!"

"Rad's instincts were right," Pacer said to a yawning Dev, who never rose before three in the afternoon. "He did tail her. And there's another one too."

"Damn, I'll have to go with you then. Actually, I need a nap." Dev pushed himself away from the wall opposite the gate for the Barbados flight.

"Fool," Pacer said as they walked swiftly toward the gate. "Why don't you try living a normal life?"

"Tell me what's normal, I may give it a shot. You know, you left my Lamborghini in a yellow zone."

"Sorry ab— Uh-oh. Let's hustle. He's grabbed her arm, and he may hurt her."

"Damn, Rad'll have our eyes if she's hurt."

The two men darted into the gate area, dodging around various passengers, who turned to gape at them. Dev collared the man who was holding Heller's arm while Pacer flung the other man to one side like a rag doll. He bowed to Heller. "Pardon us, beautiful lady. A slight inconvenience. Airports have them."

"New York has had a problem with garbage disposal," Dev said sweetly, "but these clods won't bother you anymore."

Heller looked into four dangerous eyes and mumbled a thank-you. "I have to go now."

"Yes, we certainly do," Desi said. "What the hell is going on, Heller? Who are these people? And who are those people?"

"Never mind, Desi." Heller cringed when she saw how they were being stared at. "Let's get on the plane."

Pacer turned to the two men as Heller disappeared down the jetway. "Now, let's have a little talk."

"Talk! Why were you after Miss Blane?"

Dev felt as though Pacer had asked the question a hundred times. The answers seemed to come from the expressions on their captives' faces rather than the words out of their mouths.

Bruno Domini and his henchman finally admitted that they had a score to settle with Heller Blane, but that frightening her, not harming her, had been their aim.

Some hours later, with Domini and company trying to get back to Manhattan from Westchester County, where they'd been dumped by Dev and Pacer, Con's two friends returned to Kennedy Airport and retrieved Dev's Lamborghini.

"You've been quiet, Dev."

"So have you."

"You think there's a twist here that we're missing."

"Yes."

Eight

"Calm down, Rad," Dev drawled. "We honestly don't think she's in danger." Dev's feet were propped on the inlaid rosewood desk that had belonged to Con's great-great-grandfather and was considered by some experts to be one of a kind. "Pacer's 'friends' are watching them anyway, have been these past two weeks."

"I'd feel better if I were with her." Con paced before the huge floor-to-ceiling windows that allowed a spectacular view of the Statue of Liberty. "She was almost killed in that fire."

Pacer and Dev shot quick glances at each other.

"You have to trust us, Rad," Pacer said softly. "I've never seen you really rattled—until now."

"And unhinged, hysterical, and all at sea," Con added bitterly. "She's everything to me."

"Now, that I understand," Dev muttered. He stared broodingly at the tips of his Italian loafers, as though he would lacerate the fine leather.

Pacer and Con looked at each other, then away. They were used to Dev's black moments.

The three sat or paced or doodled for fifteen minutes. When the phone rang, Con snatched up the receiver. John said it was someone for Pacer, and Con put the call on the speaker phone. "Yes?"

"Pacer? You there? It's Hippolyte. My friend, we are watching the people you talked of, and it is quiet." He paused. "It is strange to me. In many ways it is too quiet."

"What the hell?" Con thundered. Papers flew off his desk. Pacer and Dev watched him calmly.

"Easy, Rad." Pacer waited until Con nodded grimly. "Go on, Hippolyte."

"I will, Pacer." Hippolyte pronounced it "pay-say." "The talk on the street is that something is going down but I don't know what it is. We will keep working on it."

"Thanks, Hippolyte, and thanks to your 'family.' You know the drill about payment. See the man. So long."

Con punched down the intercom button. "John, get me on the next flight to Barbados." He began stuffing some papers into his briefcase.

"Looks like you're leaving us, Rad."

"Yesterday. Good-bye, gentlemen. Help yourself to the Scotch. Dinner is on me at the Andre." The door slammed behind him.

"He might fly faster than the plane by the look of him," Dev said, watching as Pacer opened the hidden bar. "He'll feel safer when he's with her."

Pacer nodded as he poured Scotch into a glass. "It's like part of Rad is gone."

"A big part, Pacer, a big part. Make that a little deeper, will you?"

"What do you think Hippolyte was talking about, Dev?"

"You mean about something going down? I wish I knew. I think we should check into that—fast."

"Right."

"Okay, Heller, does it look more realistic this way? It will look as though the heroine is running into the sea. See what I mean?"

"Yes," Heller said wearily. She glanced at her watch. It was nearly five P.M. Thank heavens. That meant they'd be quitting soon. It had been hectic consulting on this movie. She'd had no idea of the many facets of filmmaking. There were moments when she wanted nothing more than to get on a plane and race back to Con and Simeon. Her agent, Manny Levin, was delighted with the new contract that had been offered her as consultant.

"After all, Carleton Desmond has a top-drawer record on Broadway and in films," Manny told her in a long distance phone call that had crackled with static.

"I know."

It had seemed like a godsend to distance herself from Con. But now that she had begun the routine of rising at five, going over the script with Desi, the stunt people, the actors who were in the crowd scenes, discussing camera angles and the plausibility of some of the action scenes, she wasn't sure she'd done the right thing. She just hadn't counted on the fatigue factor, and there were moments when she felt completely exhausted.

"Great, Heller. That was a good idea and it fits perfectly. Okay, everybody. That's it for today."

Relieved, Heller slung her tote bag over her shoulder. She called good-bye to the various crew members near her, turning down an offer to join them for a drink at the bar in the Andre. She trudged to the golf cart the hotel had loaned her, started it up, and headed for Con's villa. He had told her she could stay there.

When she reached the villa, Heller was tempted to crawl into bed and sleep until morning. But her conscience prodded her, reminding her of her daily swim. Since she wasn't rehearsing or performing every day, she had decided she should swim in the evenings to keep in shape. Tonight she was so tired she wanted to ignore the need for exercise, but still changed into her swimsuit and walked across the beach to the sea. She could swim in the pool at the villa, but she felt in need of the sea's warm, salty balm.

She swam laps parallel to the shore, and after twenty minutes could barely lift her arms. She turned landward, and started walking as soon as her feet touched bottom. The sun was just setting, and she thought the figure she saw standing on the beach was only a strange shadow. But then she stumbled and the figure rushed toward her, and she realized who it was.

"Con!"

He splashed out to her. "What the hell do you think you're doing?"

"I was swimming. What are you doing here?"

"I came to see you. Dammit, you look like hell. What has Desi been doing to you?"

Finding a last bit of strength, she stalked past him. "Thank you very much for the charming compliment. And Desi hasn't been doing anything to me. I've just been working."

"Slaving, you mean." He grabbed her arm as she reached the beach, stopping her. "I assure you, my love, if you want to be the cause of Carleton Desmond's ruin, you're going about it the right way. I'll take him down to his socks."

"You wouldn't!" she exclaimed, but she could see the hard glitter in his eyes. He was serious. "Why do you hate Desi? He's nothing to you."

"Less than nothing. But look at you. You're exhausted. He's working you too hard. But we shouldn't stand around talking like this. I want you to get into the hot tub—"

"It's ninety degrees out here."

"And after that I want you to take a nap. I'll fix you something to eat."

"Con, I am not an invalid and you know it from the doctor's reports since you're read all of them."

"Admit you're tired to the bone."

"It was a busy day—"

"Ha! See, and that damn fool working you like a coolie."

"He isn't . . . not really."

"You worked hard enough in that show. You don't need any more strain."

"I can't walk away from this. Desi is counting on me."

"Then tell him you'll only work eight-hour days, not twelve."

She walked slowly. She'd thought of that. "You know, it's not just the work. I didn't expect the rush of memories that came with the job."

"Naturally. That fire was very traumatic."

"Desi wrote this script long before we ever met. He'd read about it in the papers. He came pretty close to the actual happenings a time or two." She smothered a yawn with her hand. "What are you doing here?"

"I wanted to be with you."

Remembering the look on Bruno Domini's face at the airport, she stared at him suspiciously. "Is that all?"

"Pacer and Dev are checking on something, but it might be nothing."

"But you don't think so."

Con hesitated. "I'm not sure." When she shuddered, he put his arms around her.

"Now that you're here, I feel better." Her voice was muffled against his chest.

"And have you enjoyed it?"

"Working as a consultant? No . . . yes. It's different, and it's been like a catharsis for me. Perhaps I needed to relive it to put it all in perspective."

"I won't make waves if you promise to take it very easy." He took her arm and led her to the outdoor hot tub. "The water will relax you." When he would have pulled the strap of her suit from her shoulder, she pushed his hand away. "Don't be silly, Heller. I've seen you without clothes."

"I'll still wear my suit."

"No need to be shy with me." He shrugged, stripped off his own brief suit, and stepped into the tub with her.

Damn the man! she thought. It wasn't fair that he should have such a beautiful body. How Apollo would have hated Conrad Wendel!

The waves of warm water massaged and rocked her body. Soon she was mesmerized by the motion of the water . . . and Con's touch.

*   *   *

Con watched her slide sideways, panic feathering through him at how quickly she slept. Maybe he should call a doctor. When he was certain she was deeply asleep, he lifted her out of the tub and carried her into the master suite. He stripped off her swimsuit and dried her gently, then placed her between the silk sheets.

For several minutes he sat beside the bed, watching her. She was sleeping peacefully, naturally. He hated the idea of anything being wrong with her, yet he figured it wasn't necessary to call a doctor. She just needed sleep. He kissed her lightly on the forehead and left.

An hour later he was in the living room of the master suite going over some files he'd brought with him, when he heard her stirring. He dropped his papers on the floor and strode into the room.

"You're awake," he said.

She turned her head toward him, blinking. "Yes." She pushed herself up on her elbows. "My goodness, I really slept."

He smiled as he walked toward the bed. "Crazy woman," he said affectionately. "You need someone to take care of you."

"Did you have someone in mind?" she asked.

"Yes." He stopped beside the bed and stared down at her. "Me. We're getting married."

Her smile was blinding in its brilliance. "I'd like that very much," she said softly.

The iron bands of tension and fear that had bound him since the morning he'd woken up alone in the Andre Hotel finally slipped away. "Oh, God, Heller." He sat down on the bed and grasped her hands, then lifted them to his lips. "I love you, Heller, and when you're my wife, I'll be a very happy man."

"And I'll be a very happy woman."

He leaned down to kiss her, and neither spoke again for a long time.

"I thought we might dine at the Plantation this evening," Con said as he dressed.

Heller nodded, content to leave things in his hands. She was still in bed, luxuriating in the feel of the silk sheets and the memory of Con's lovemaking. "I really like the lobster tail there, though it's big enough to feed a small family."

"And you'll have no trouble finishing it."

"You're not exactly shy when it comes to stoking your furnace, Mr. Wendel."

"No, I'm not." He leaned down and kissed her hard.

"I've done a great deal of thinking down here."

"Oh, and have you come to any conclusions?"

"Some things are clear, others are not."

"Like the Domini brothers?"

She nodded. "I was so scared when I saw Domini at the airport. Thank you for sending Pacer and Dev along."

"I knew you were still scared, and that worried me."

"You know, it was strange. That was the first time he had ever approached me personally. Before my mother and I went into the WPP, he'd always done his threatening over the phone."

Con frowned, trying not to show his concern. "You don't have to worry about him now. My lawyer has pushed the district attorney into charging Domini for harassing you."

"Is that wise, Con? Look what happened to my mother and me because she felt she had to do her civic duty."

"That won't happen again. Pacer has contacted a few people he knows, and so has Dev. Neither one of the brothers is eager to return to jail . . . or be killed."

"Con!"

"I will take any and all steps to protect you, Heller. You will never have to look over your shoulder again."

"You are a barbarian, Con," she said softly.

"I've discovered new depths in myself since meeting you."

"Tell me about you, Dev, and Pacer in Vietnam."

He looked down at the sheet, picking at the silky richness. "That was a quick change. What do you want to know?"

"Everything."

His head whipped up and he stared hard at her. "That would take years."

"Tell me some now, please."

"We had always been together at Princeton and it seemed natural to go. None of us had any idea of the horror until we were in the thick of it. Dev was a hell-for-leather hero type, Pacer was quieter, quick, and sure, but no less brave. All three of us were wounded at one time or another."

Heller watched his face. It had paled from the painful memories, though his tone was matter-of-fact. "You have a scar on your back. . . ."

"Why darling, I'm so pleased you remembered." He chuckled. "I was caught in a crossfire. It took a while to get out."

Heller knew that it would take many long years to pry the whole story from him, but she meant to try. Con had been her support; she wanted to be his. "You're putting me off. Is it so difficult to discuss?"

"Yeah, in a way it still is. I don't have as many nightmares anymore, but I do know that some of my fellow soldiers had little to come back to when it was over. Two of our friends live in the wilds of Wyoming. The three of us have been out there to see Deek and Joe a couple of times, and believe me when I tell you that their everyday life is as tough as combat survival."

Heller put her hand on his. "I guess no one who hasn't been there can really appreciate it."

He turned her hand over and kissed the palm. "Maybe not, but I do feel very comfortable talking to you about it and I can't say that about my own family."

"You have a nice family."

"Thank you. They like you too. My mother is looking forward to the time when you're her daughter-in-law and she can catalogue all my faults to you."

"We'd have to live two lifetimes to get them all in, I'm sure. Ouch, you bit my thumb." It hadn't hurt, but it was better to fuss about it than melt like a piece of chocolate in the sun.

"I'm sorry, I didn't think I was hurting you." His lazy smile told her he saw right through her. "Shall I get in there with you and comfort you?"

"No. I have to get dressed." She pulled the sheet up to her nose. "Which means you have to leave."

He leaned down, plucked the sheet back with one finger, and kissed her. His tongue forced its way between her lips, dueling with hers until her rising passion threatened to send her through the roof.

He tore his mouth away. "Bye," he said, and strolled from the room.

Heller stared after him, too weak to move. "Beast," she gasped.

Con remained standing in the hall for a few moments, then strode decisively into the den. He walked over to the large scrolled desk that he'd found in a ruined building in Barbados and had refinished, and picked up the phone to call the Plantation. "Hello, this is Con Wendel. I'd like to make a reservation for this evening for two, eight o'clock. By the way, could you tell me if there's a way to marry quickly in these islands without going through a great deal of red tape? Tambori? I don't think I've ever heard of it. It's part of the Windward Islands? How long a flight? Good. Oh, wait, can you give me a minister to call or . . . Ah, I see, Government House. Thank you."

It was too late to get hold of anyone now, but he made a note to call Government House on Tambori first thing in the morning.

"Have you been thinking that maybe this could be a smoke screen, Pacer?"

"About every other minute."

"Somebody could be after Rad and would find this a convenient way to cover his tracks. The two of them caught together, both down, everyone would think it was because of Heller."

Pacer nodded. He picked up the phone and quickly dialed a number. "It's Pacer Dillon, sir. Could we talk to you? Yes, this afternoon, privately."

That afternoon the two men walked into Colonel Simon Wendel's office.

"All right you two, what is it?" It wasn't Simon's habit to take anyone on trust, but he had never doubted that the two men in front of him had his son's best interests at heart.

In terse sentences the two sketched out what they thought could be happening to Con, what they knew, and what they surmised.

Simon listened to the end, his fingers steepled in front of him as he leaned back in his chair. "So you think someone could be after Conrad?"

"Yes, sir."

Simon stared first at one then at the other. "If it's something that he hasn't noticed, it could be because it's too close to him and obscures his vision."

"You're a very canny man, sir," Pacer said. "That's what we decided as well. Has anyone around him had access to either his company's or his private accounts? Could someone be skimming in the business or on a private scale?"

"Sir," Dev said when the older man frowned with concern, "it would have to be someone very close to him, someone he sees all the time, not necessarily the family."

Simon nodded, his index finger rubbing down the side of his nose. "I'll make a few inquiries."

"And we'll do the same with some sources we have, sir, unless you'd object."

"No objection. I want the truth—and fast. I don't like the feeling that someone is stalking my son, or Heller, whether psychologically or literally."

"We don't like it much either, sir," Pacer said. The pencil he'd been fiddling with splintered in his hand. "Sorry about that, sir. Don't like to make a mess."

"No problem." Some of the worry left Simon as he studied the two men sprawled in chairs on the opposite side of his desk. They were about as relaxed as spitting cobras. Con was in good hands.

The wedding at Government House on Tambori was brief and simple but Heller thought it was beautiful. Afterward she wasn't able to take her eyes off the intricately worked diamond ring that had substituted for a wedding band.

"I have my eye on matching plain bands for us," Con said, "but I've been carrying this around to give to you as an engagement ring. Today it did double duty."

"I love it. Thank you, Con."

"Thank you, wife of mine, for marrying me. You've given me a great gift."

"I love you, Con."

"I love you and need you, Heller Wendel."

They flew back to New York a few days later, when Desi no longer needed Heller's help. During the flight Con noticed Heller kept sending him quick, searching glances whenever she thought he wasn't looking. "If you have a question darling, ask away."

"Con, will you mind my being on the stage now?"

"No more than I have from the start." He kissed her ring finger. "I want you to express yourself and be happy in your work, Heller . . . even if it is as a stripper."

"Would you like children, other than Simeon?"

"As soon as you're able to have one safely. I would

like a girl first, with blond hair and turquoise eyes. I'll want her to be called Heller."

"Junior? Should we do that to her?"

Con watched the sunshine radiate out of her. "We'll be a family."

She nodded. "We could call a girl after our mothers instead."

"If you want that, darling, then we'll do it."

"Sarah was my mother's middle name. Sarah Melanie would be beautiful."

"If it's a boy, I think we'll have to reconsider."

She laughed, reaching for his hand and threading her fingers through his.

Delight filled his being at her obvious joy. Making Heller happy brought him a happiness he'd never known.

Nine

Con was used to moving mountains in business and cutting through red tape. Traveling was no different. He expected and got the best service. So when he was given VIP treatment deplaning from the commercial flight, he thought nothing of it.

"You're not the blooming king, you know," Heller whispered as two men dashed forward to grab their luggage off the baggage carousel.

Con shot her a sharp glance, then smiled. "Pay no attention, darling. If I didn't think you'd hit me, I'd have a red carpet put down in front of your every step."

"Don't be silly—" She broke off when she saw the determined glitter in his eyes. "Sometimes you're crazy," she said softly.

Con turned to give directions to the porter carrying Heller's suitcases, when his attention was caught by Pacer and Dev heading his way at a dead run.

Con didn't need their shouts of warning. Automatically he shoved Heller behind him and crouched. "Stay down. Don't move." Eyes scanning the crowds, he saw a man lift a Sten gun. Fear laced him at the thought of what the spray of the automatic hand-gun could do. Even while it was coming up, he reached for an umbrella on a luggage cart. "Every-body down," he shouted, then stood and tossed the only missile he had. The man dodged it, then aimed again.

"No, Con, don't!" Heller cried when she saw Con ready himself to lunge. "No, no, no. Con!"

Seemingly in slow motion he hurtled toward the man who could hurt or maim Heller. Fear gave him impetus as he imagined life without her. His body flew through the air as though he could stop the deadly projectiles coming from the gun.

Dev dropped to one knee, his own gun trained on the man. It was too far.

"Drop him. Don't miss, old buddy," Pacer whis-pered just before he fired. "Damn, you got him right in the ear, my man. Very clean shooting, I must say. Glad to see that some of your skills haven't been lost in drinking and wenching."

"My skills are honed just that way, old buddy. That was some tackle of Rad's, wasn't it?" Dev walked unhurriedly toward his friend, who was lying atop the dead gunman.

"He was always athletic as hell," Pacer said. Look-ing around, he saw security guards with their guns drawn running toward Conrad. He moved to inter-cept them.

As Dev reached him, Conrad scrambled up and turned toward Heller. She was running toward him, her arms outstretched.

"Con, Con!"

She flung herself at him and he caught her. "Shh, it's all over, darling, truly it is."

"Oh, Con, this wouldn't' have happened if you hadn't been with me. The Domini brothers haven't forgotten."

"Shh, Heller, don't cry that way, darling, it's over."

"And it wasn't you he was after, Heller," Dev said, slipping his gun into the shoulder holster under his coat.

Con turned toward his friend, with Heller still in his arms. "That was some shot, chum."

"You should have trusted me to do it, Rad. Not leapt like that into the line of fire."

"I couldn't take a chance." He tightened his hold on Heller. "What was that you said about it not being Heller?"

"It wasn't Heller he was after. We think you've been the target for a while now. The Domini brothers are too scared to face the anger of certain persons. No, we don't know who's behind it, but we will."

"Yes, we will." Pacer ambled up to them and sent Dev an ironic look. "I could wish you weren't quite so good a shot. We can't question this guy."

"Did you take care of the authorities?" Con asked.

'Yep, but they'll be out to your place to ask a few questions."

"Fine. I want to get Heller home now."

Heller didn't budge, her eyes on Dev. "Are you saying that someone is trying to kill Con?"

Dev grinned at Con's hard look. "Wing him, maybe. Don't worry, ma'am. He owes us money. We won't let anything happen to him."

"Neither will I," Heller promised, stepping closer to him.

Noticing her thrust-out jaw, her clenched fists, Con grinned. "Are you going to be my protector?"

"Darn right."

"Hot damn, Rad," Pacer said. "You are one lucky fella. I think I might chance married life with such as Miss Heller Blane."

"You're right about that, Pace," Dev drawled, his gaze roaming over Heller. "You have one prize lady."

Con glared at his two friends. "I know that."

"I do believe he might kill us, Dev," Pacer said serenely.

"I think you're right," Dev answered sweetly.

"This is no time for levity," Heller said. "We have to find the people responsible for this, and right away."

"Yes, ma'am," Pacer said. "Don't look so ferocious. We've been on it, I promise."

"I don't want this happening to him again."

"We'll do our level best," Dev said solemnly. "Shall we get out of here? I think your father will want to know about this, Rad. Why don't I call him and we'll— What's the matter? Something come to mind?"

"It might not be that easy to isolate those who knew about my trip, starting with my company, my family, and assorted friends," Con mused aloud, then his glance went to Heller and he shrugged. "Let's get moving."

Heller stayed put. "Don't shut me out, Con. You didn't like it when you thought I was doing it to you."

"The lady is right, Rad," Pacer said.

"All right, Heller. You'll know everything we know."

Once in the limousine, Con cuddled her close to him. "It was a sudden decision to go to Barbados, but I don't kid myself that it was a secret."

"Life in the fast lane has its drawbacks," Dev said, his satirical tone belied by the worry in his eyes. "We may have to do some fancy digging."

"I'm good with a shovel," Pacer said.

"No one is getting to Con." Heller stared hard at the two friends of the man she'd come to love so much.

"Agreed." Dev's dark eyes lightened when they settled on the ring on her left hand.

Quickly Con explained it was a substitute for the wedding bands he hadn't had time to buy.

"May I offer my felicitations to both of you?" Dev asked.

Pacer grinned and pumped Con's hand before kissing Heller. "It's great that you two got married, but I always figured we would be with you when you did this, Rad."

"So did I, but I was in a hurry to tie up the lady."

"Smart man," Dev said softly. Then he, too, shook Con's hand and kissed Heller. "Be happy." The doleful eyes narrowed as though his thoughts were traveling rapidly back in time.

Con pressed a button and a phone console appeared. "I'm going to call the office and have John alert security."

"Is that John Taylor, your assistant?" Dev consulted some notes on his lap. "He has quite a background. Rhodes scholar, doctoral thesis on van Gogh. He should be teaching in a university."

Con nodded. "He's very bright. My mother and he have the deepest conversations on art. John has helped her out more than once in that way. He's purchased a few good things himself. He was lucky enough to receive a sizable legacy from an uncle, and that's given him some leeway in collecting art. And he knows his job with Wendel's too."

"Oh? Is that the way you invest, Rad? Art?"

"Sometimes." He shot a hard look at the notebook on Pacer's lap. "Are you keeping a dossier on everyone I know?"

"Yes." Dev and Pacer answered at the same time.

"Now, look—"

"Never mind, Con. I think they're doing the right thing," Heller said firmly. "Keep going, you two. I'll tell you anything you want to know."

"There's no need, darling." Con pulled her closer to him.

"We already know most of it, ma'am," Pacer said. "You and your mama had quite a time of it." His smile was crooked. "Always admired guts." He gently touched the back of her hand.

"Thank you."

"We're working our way through the family too, Rad," Dev said. "And us."

"It must be a family member then, because it isn't either of you," Con said softly, kissing the top of Heller's head.

"That's not funny," Heller muttered. "There must be something you're missing."

The two friends nodded, then step by step they outlined what they had been doing, whom they'd contacted, and which people they'd added to their suspect list, and which they'd removed.

Heller looked up in surprise when they stopped in front of the Wendel Building in lower Manhattan. "That was fast."

"We should have taken the copter," Conrad muttered.

"No," Pacer said. "You were more protected this way. Sorry, ma'am. I sure don't want to upset you."

"You haven't upset me, Pacer. I just don't want to be kept out of things."

"Yes, ma'am."

The private elevator sped them to the penthouse. They stepped right into Con's private office. The outer office door opened and John Taylor poked in his head, looking taken aback.

"I didn't expect you here today, sir." John coughed to clear his throat.

"How are you, John? Wish me happy, will you. Heller and I are married."

Surprise kept John immobile for a moment, then he smiled and crossed the room, congratulating the couple.

"Hold all calls, John," Con said, "unless it's an emergency. We're going to be in conference for a while. Send in some soup and fruit in a little while, and coffee."

John nodded and left, closing the door behind him.

"I'd like to use the powder room, Con," Heller said.

He took a key from his top desk drawer and handed it to her. "Go through to the apartment I keep here. You can come back the same way, or there's another door that leads into the main hall if you want to explore. Just don't go too far." He kissed her quickly. "I'll miss you."

"Fool," she whispered, and left, ignoring the low laughter from the other two.

When Heller stepped from the office into the apartment, she had to gasp. The fully furnished apartment was large, with a living room, a bedroom, and a study. The bathroom was enormous, with a separate shower stall and even a sauna.

Looking around after using the facilities, she decided there was a great deal about Con she didn't know. But one thing she was sure of was that he was a man of taste. The paintings on the walls of the living room were a melange of periods and taste, running from Cezanne and Monet to Sargent to Rothko.

Becoming more curious about the man she had come to love, she wandered about the apartment, breathing in the essence of the man. Con's stamp was everywhere.

She decided to return to Con's office via the more roundabout route. Walking down the main hall, she saw a door marked Private. Thinking it was Con's office, she was surprised when she opened the door and saw John Taylor. He looked very intent, working on his computer. Loath to disturb him, she was about to back out into the hall, when he looked up and spotted her. He blinked in surprise before he smiled.

"Hello. Are you lost?"

"I hope not. I was just going back to Con's office from the apartment. It's a beautiful apartment."

John nodded. "And it comes in handy when we have an all-night negotiating session or something. You can get to Mr. Wendel's office right through here." He gestured to the door beyond his desk.

"Thank you." He rose to open the door for her, but she paused. "Wait."

"Yes?"

"You're very loyal to Con, I know." When John nodded, she continued. "Would you keep a closer watch on him? We have reason to think that someone is trying to—hurt him."

John stiffened. "Of course I will. So that's why Mr. Abrams and Mr. Dillon are with him."

Heller nodded. "Thank you."

"Don't worry, Mrs. Wendel. I can take some steps to insure that he's well protected while he's here." He opened the door and she walked into Con's office.

"There you are, darling. How did you like the apartment? Come and sit down next to me." Con was sitting on a sofa across the room from his desk. Pacer and Dev were in armchairs opposite the low table in front of the sofa.

"The apartment is lovely," she said as she sat down, "but the art is what fascinates me." She drew in a deep breath. "I'd rather discuss what the three of you plan to do as precautionary measures."

She listened as the men discussed their plans, both for protecting her and Con and for discovering who was trying to harm them. After a while she began to get sleepy, the effects of the long flight catching up with her. More than once she had to smother a yawn.

"That's enough," Con finally said. "Heller's exhausted. We need to nap. Right, darling?" He grinned at her as the other two men chuckled.

"You are a lecher, Conrad Wendel." But she smiled too.

"Come along, darling, I'll take you home."

Heller was glad to return to the stage, but a week after her return from Barbados she had to let her stand-in go on for her.

Con's parents were throwing a celebration party in honor of their marriage. Heller was nervous.

"You're crazy to be jumpy about this," Doodie told her. She and Leonard had come to the Wendels' apartment so they could all go to the party together.

"Look how calm I am and I'm going to be telling everyone that I was the designated maid of honor." Doodie grinned and whirled around in front of her friend. "I love this dress. Leonard says I'm dynamite in it. I hope you'll be back from your trip in time for my wedding, Heller. Con says he's taking you to a secret place."

"We intend to be at your wedding with bells on, all three Wendels—Con, Simeon, and I." Heller hugged her friend.

"I'm planning on having a baby right away. Leonard is so taken with Simeon, he might try to kidnap him."

"He is a wonderful boy, isn't he? He and Con are developing such a good relationship."

"Maybe not now." Doodie grinned. "While you were showering, both Leonard and Con started to go on dressing Simeon. He was balking."

"Couldn't get him out of jeans. Right?"

"Something like that. He said that his clothes were choking him." Doodie looked her friend up and down and shook her head. "You should be registered with the police in that outfit."

"What do you mean? The neckline is high, the hem's only a couple of inches above the knee—"

"And the back is cut to the coccyx," Doodie interjected dryly. "I wish I could wear it, but with legs that look like umbrella stands, it's not a good choice."

"You were voted the prettiest girl in our class."

"I was younger then. Now I'm waffling from my eyebrows to my big toe."

"And Leonard is always commenting on your sexy figure."

"I'm marrying a darling. He never sees the obvious."

"Doodie! Stop it." Heller laughed, knowing her friend was totally confident in her relationship with her fiancé. "You look wonderful in that sapphire shade."

"It's my best color. Shall we join the men and see if Simeon has convinced Con and Leonard to wear jeans?"

As they walked toward Simeon's bedroom on the other side of the apartment, they could hear laughter.

"What's going on here?" Doodie called. "Ohh, Simeon, you're gorgeous."

Simeon looked from Doodie to Heller. "Very pretty."

The two women hugged him, and the men chuckled.

"Shouldn't do that to us, old fellow," Leonard said. "We're supposed to be teaching you how to handle women."

"Oh, Simeon," Heller said, leaning down to him. "That was so clear. Can you say my name like that?"

Simeon nodded.

"Do it."

"Hel-ler."

"Yes, yes, that's right. Soon your name will be Simeon Wendel. Will you like that?"

"Ma-ma and Dad." Simeon beamed when Heller and Doodie fumbled for handkerchiefs.

"You should stop doing that to them, son." Con hugged the boy himself. "You'll be a smash in the business world."

"I'd like him to be an archaeologist," Doodie said dreamily, dabbing at her eyes.

"Or a geologist," Heller said, sniffling into her tissue.

"What's wrong with being a college professor?" Leonard asked. "Or a symphony conductor? My mother will try to talk him into that."

"My mother will want him to be a chiropodist," Conrad said dryly. "She wants miracle feet in her lifetime with no calluses."

Heller laughed. "I have a good mind to repeat that to your family."

"They will only corroborate what I say, darling." His smile faded as he stared at her. "You are too sexy to take anywhere," he muttered, pulling her close and wiping her eyes. "I think I smeared your makeup, sweet. Cross with me?"

She shook her head, wanting to stay in his arms, wanting to keep him safe with her. There was danger out there for him, and she had great difficulty with that. Somehow it hadn't seemed so bad when it had been her problem. The blood congealed in her veins at the thought of someone menacing Con.

"Are you feeling all right?" he asked.

"What?" She shook her head. "I was just thinking."

"Are you sure? You're a little pale."

"I'm fine." He was too astute, as usual, reading her thoughts with no problem.

"You're too beautiful." He kissed her nose.

"Kissing. Ugh!" Simeon said as clearly as a bell, making the adults look at him with wonder and amusement.

"Well, I'm going to kiss you, Simeon, every chance I get," Heller said. She freed herself from Con and hugged the boy again.

"Me too," Doodie said, her arms enfolding him as well.

"For someone who is doing a great deal of wriggling, he doesn't seem to mind the ladies fussing over him," Leonard said to Con.

Con chuckled. "The boy's no fool. Come along, all of you, it's time to go."

The ride out to Long Island was long, but none of the adults minded. Con had made sure their limousine came equipped with champagne.

When they finally turned into the drive of the Wendel estate Simeon sat forward in his seat next to the chauffeur and gasped. "Castle!"

"It does look like one," Doodie said uneasily. "I hope my dress is all right."

"You look lovely, Doodie. My family will be honored to know you," Con said in a courtly manner.

As they were helped from the car, Doodie whispered to Heller, "you should call him Sir Galahad, not Conrad."

Heller smiled, wishing she could tell Doodie she was a little apprehensive herself, but she didn't want to add to her friend's discomfort.

"See, there was no need for you to be nervous about this evening," Con said to them both as the family converged on Simeon. "I think our son is a born showman, don't you? Look at him handle my mother."

"He's come far from that fearful life he was living before."

"To the manner born."

She looked over her shoulder at Con. "Do you know how many of your mannerisms he's adopted?"

Con looked startled, then pleased. "Has he? Which, for instance?"

"That habit you have of touching your chin when you're ruminating."

"Ruminating? Come on, darling, when was the last time you saw me chewing my cud?"

"An hour ago, I think."

He laughed and pulled her tight to him. His mouth hovered above hers. "Will I smear?"

"They tell me it's foolproof," she said huskily.

His mouth settled on hers, his tongue parting her lips. When he lifted his head, his breathing was ragged.

"Con, my boy," his father said, approaching them, "I could wish I ever had half as much power over you as Heller does. How are you, my dear? You look stunning." He put his arm around her. "And may I say, welcome to the family."

"Evening, Father," Con said.

"Thank you, sir," Heller said. "How are you?"

"I am fine, my dear." He lifted her left hand. "I see you're wearing my mother's ring. It looks beautiful on you. How happy she'll be to see it on your hand." He grinned. "But my wife might turn green. My mother is rather a curmudgeon and she always makes life rocky for my Mel, even insisting that she never wear her ring when she knows Mel loves it."

"Oh, but, sir." Heller tugged at the ring, but Simon covered her hand. "I don't mind giving it to your wife."

"I mind," Con said brusquely.

"Con!" She stared at him askance as his father laughed.

"It's your ring," Con said. "It belongs to you. Whether my sister or mother wants it is immaterial."

"Your sister wants it too?" Heller was dumbfounded. "I won't be a bone of contention between you and your family." Again she struggled to remove the ring.

Con looked irritated and tightly held her hands. "That is your ring, Heller."

"Truly, it is," Simon said. "My tyrant of a mother wouldn't have it any other way. Do you mind if I tag along when you speak to the others?"

"Father!"

"Sorry, Con, I just wanted to see their reactions." Simon grinned unrepentantly. "Come along and greet your mother."

"We should leave," Con muttered.

"You can't," his father said. "All your friends are here to celebrate your marriage."

"Getting married in a private ceremony was the best idea I've ever had."

"You look like a bear with a sore paw, Con." Simon laughed, earning a scowl from his son.

"Enjoying yourself, sir?" Pacer asked. He and Dev had soundlessly walked up behind Con and Heller.

"Indeed I am." Simon slapped the two men on their backs, then urged his son to bring Heller to his mother before ambling away.

"He's full of himself tonight," Con said. He looked at his two friends. "Was Father apprised of everything that happened?"

"He's relieved that you and Heller are back in this country," Dev said. "He's sure nothing can happen to you here." He dropped a kiss on Heller's cheek. "Keep him in line, love."

"I'm buying a whip and a chair," she said.

"I'd suggest an M1 and a rocket launcher," Pacer said.

"Very amusing," Con said. "You two can stay with us when we greet the family."

"No thanks, I'll visit the bar." Dev was about to move, when Heller took hold of his arm. "Now, Heller, honey, you don't need us."

"His mother always wanted my ring," she said in a weak voice. "She'll hate me now."

"Won't either," Pacer said. "She's an angel, is Mrs. W. Wait until you get to know her."

"She loves us," Dev drawled.

As they aproached the older woman, Heller hung back, but finally she was facing Con's mother.

"How lovely you look, Heller, like a modern Venus." She spied the ring and closed her eyes as though wincing. "I suppose my husband told you to confront me. The animal, where is he?"

"Right behind you, love." Simon laughed.

"That's right, be amused at my expense, just like that old termagant." She smiled ruefully at Heller. "I loved Con on sight, but I regretted his birth because my old dragon of a mother-in-law wanted an heir so badly." Melanie sighed deeply. "That ring looks wonderful on you, dear, and certainly suits your hand better than mine." She held out her hand. An enormous sapphire ring graced it, and she brightened when she looked at the stone. "And she was nearly apoplectic when she saw this ring . . . oh, dear, here she comes. I keep hoping that she'll be too tired to attend one of these." Melanie's company smile was a bit forced as she turned to greet her mother-in-law. "Mother Wendel, how are you?"

"Better than you, Mellie. You wear too much makeup and you could use some trimming. You look like a battleship going away." The elderly woman cackled when she saw blood run up her daughter-in-law's face. "I was always thin."

"With a neck like a chicken," Melanie said, her chin up, her eyes flashing.

"Did you hear your wife, Simon? She insulted me."

"No, she didn't, Mother, she retaliated, which she wouldn't have to do if you didn't bait her." Simon gently kissed his mother's forehead.

She was distracted by a friend, and Simon turned

around to kiss his wife on the mouth. "I'm going to get you a ruby ring tomorrow."

"Oh, Simon." Melanie laughed. "Why do I let her get to me? I should learn."

"I've told you to pay no attention, dearest."

"I think you're probably the greatest source of happiness she has, Mrs. Wendel," Heller said, then felt a flutter of shyness when everyone looked at her. Con's mother gaped at her.

"Whatever do you mean, Heller?"

"I'll bet she needs the stimulation of sparring with you. And perhaps she isn't the type of person who could say straight out how proud she is of her grandchildren and how grateful she is to you for producing them." Con kissed the back of her neck as Melanie turned to her husband.

"What do you think, Simon?"

"I think our daughter-in-law is very perceptive." He took Heller's hand and led her over to his formidable mother. "Mother, this is Heller."

"Atrocious name. Parents didn't like you?"

Heller gazed in astonishment at the imposing matriarch, then laughter escaped her. She couldn't stem the mirth that rolled from her.

Her mouth drooping slightly, Maribel Hunter Wendel stared at Heller, then her lips twitched and she, too, began to laugh. "Saw right through me, did you?"

"Yes, ma'am. My mother was very spunky."

"Must have passed it on to you."

"I'd like to think she did."

"She did, Grandmother." Con kissed his wife on the neck again. "May I escort you lovely ladies into the ballroom?"

"Nope," his grandmother responded grandly. She

gestured imperiously to Dev and Pacer. "I'll go with these two. I don't like to share my men."

"I know the feeling," Heller said softly, earning another smile from the matriarch as she was escorted away. Heller turned to Con. "Now I know where you picked up the arrogance, but I do like her."

"You should have met her husband. He was the most outspoken man I've ever known but canny enough to have made several fortunes in his lifetime."

"What a family you have."

"Yes. Shall we dance?"

She nodded, eager to be held in his arms. He was being attentive, but she could tell something preoccupied him.

The evening became a blur as partner after partner claimed Heller for a dance.

Finally freeing herself, she walked over to Simeon, who was pondering an array of finger food on a sideboard. "Hi. How would you like to dance with your mother?"

Simeon shook his head. "Don't know how."

"I'll show you. Will you try?" She was a little surprised when the boy assented. He had come out of so many shells.

On the dance floor he was very solemn, his one hand at her waist, the other clutching her hand.

"Don't look at the floor, darling. That's right. It's just fine to count out loud. Whoops, the music changed, that's a fast one. Simeon! Where did you learn to do that?" Heller laughed as the boy gyrated in front of her, his thin body bending and swaying to the rock beat.

Imitating his moves, Heller joined him and they danced around the floor, totally unaware they were being watched.

"She is something special, Rad," Dev said to Con, who was staring intensely at Heller.

"Yes. And it doesn't comfort me to know that some-one at this party could be watching her, waiting to hurt her because she's part of me."

"Easy, man. Pacer and I are pretty sure it's you who's the target, not Heller. What would be the sense of going after her? She knows nothing about your business. No, you're the one they want, old friend."

"Really? And what better way to get at me than through her? Nothing could immobilize me as much."

Dev straightened, looking from the laughing Heller and Simeon to his friend. Then his sharp gaze shot around the room. "You think your nemesis is here?"

"I don't know, but he's been able to get mighty close to me and to her, time after time."

Dev nodded to Pacer on the other side of the room. Casually, Pacer made his way to them.

"Trouble?"

"Rad says the nemesis is here."

"That a fact?"

"Whoever it is, we get him tonight."

"I think we should."

Dev gave his friend an acid smile, incongruous in his congenial visage.

He had watched the two of them out there laugh-ing and dancing and it made him want to grind his teeth. Instead, he smiled and looked interested as he gazed around the opulent room. Why should they have it all? He was entitled to some, and he was going to get it. Treading softly was the answer, not making waves. Controlling the situation was the most important thing to do.

The woman was the focus. She had already provided him with enough ammunition to get the ball rolling.

Once he had her, the rest would be easy. He knew she was going to adopt the boy, so he could be useful too. He would use every tool at his disposal, apply any leverage required. This time he wouldn't be stopped. Too much was at stake. He'd lost too much and now stood to gain it all back . . . and more.

Moving swiftly, he slipped out the door at the far end of the ballroom. He knew the property well enough to get around, and the lanterns placed strategically in the English-style garden would provide ample illumination.

He walked rapidly around the stone terrace that girdled the house and saw the woman and the boy come out onto the terrace, talking and laughing. Where they stood, the terrace bellied out into a dining area overlooking the formal gardens.

Glancing in the windows, he took a deep breath. He had only a few minutes. Conrad Wendel kept a close watch on his woman and the boy. He would come looking for them shortly.

Heller and the boy didn't notice him even when he was quite close. They were leaning over the parapet talking about the flowers. It really might be more efficient to kill them than blackmail Wendel. Umm, that would take some thought. Would there be any way to handle Wendel if something happened to his wife?

". . . and those tall, colorful ones waving in the breeze are dahlias."

"They have faces."

Heller laughed. "It looks that way, doesn't it?"

"Mrs. Wendel, Mr. Wendel would like to see you down by the gazebo. He said I was to show you the way. Will you come with me, please. And of course bring Simeon."

"All right. How are you, John? It must be a treat for you to have the evening off after a hard day at the office."

"Treat? Yes, I suppose you could say that."

Heller caught the tightness in his voice. "Is something wrong, John?"

"No, not at all. It's just that Mr. Wendel was adamant that you join him as soon as possible."

"All right, but the heels of my shoes are going to sink into the ground and slow us up. Come along, Simeon,"

"Mama doesn't have to hurry," Simeon told John brusquely, taking Heller's hand protectively.

"He's very possessive of you, isn't he?"

Heller blinked at John's tone of voice and slowed her steps. "I think we'll go back to the ballroom, John. You can tell Con that we'll meet him—John, what are you doing? Let him go!" Immobilized for a moment when John put a choke hold on Simeon, Heller threw herself at the man, tearing at his hand.

"Back off, you damned she-cat, or I'll break his neck. I mean it."

"Mama, run."

"If you do, I'll twist his head off his shoulders."

"I'm not moving. Don't hurt him, please."

"Get going. Follow the winding path, the down one, not the up, and hurry. I'll be right behind you with the boy."

Heller toyed with the idea of running, screaming, turning and fighting, but the fear of what John could do to Simeon kept her moving forward.

The gazebo was far from the house and somewhat isolated. The sides were enclosed with latticework, enabling the inhabitants to see out but not allowing outsiders to see in. It was lighted all around with recessed pinkish lighting that gave it a surrealistic glow.

Once inside, Heller turned to face John. "What do you want? We have nothing of interest to you. Tell me what this is about."

"You are going to provide access to the Wendel art collection. If things work out, you and the boy won't be harmed. If there are problems, you will be expendable."

Ten

Con was more than uneasy. He was angry and wary.

"You mustn't worry if she's out of your sight for just a moment," his mother said, "though I can see why you cherish her. She is a dear girl."

"You say that because she just explained my mother to you," Simon said, though he was worriedly scanning the cluster of guests in the large ballroom.

"She shed some insight for you too, Simon. Whatever are you craning your neck for, dear? You're as bad as Con. Ah, here come Pacer and Dev. Why are they shaking their heads and looking so grim? Do you suppose they're miffed with me for having them dance with the Alnot sisters, Simon?"

"No, dearest, it wouldn't be that. Why don't you go and smile sweetly at my mother and throw her off stride?"

"Are you trying to get rid of me? Is something wrong?" Melanie's eyes widened as she gazed at the grim expressions on the faces of her son, son-in-law, and husband. "Has something happened to Heller?"

"No, dear, and we're going to make sure that nothing does."

"Good." Melanie smiled shakily. "I do like her, and Simeon is our grandchild, or soon will be."

"Sweetheart, don't fret. I promise you that Simeon will be sailing and playing tennis at our place all summer. Now, go and see to Mother."

"I love you, Simon. Be careful." She kissed her husband, then touched her son's arm. "Find her, dearest boy."

"I will, Mother, and right now." Con gestured for the other four men to cluster close around him. "Alert security. No one would have gotten by Tabor and his people without question. Father and Will, you stay here and keep your eyes open. Dev, you and Pace come with me. We'll check the grounds. She was with Simeon, so maybe she's showing him the garden."

"We'll find her, Rad," Dev said, and the other men nodded.

Con, Dev, and Pacer slipped out of the house and across the terrace to the enormous grounds that stretched out behind the mansion. Con noticed that not too many of the women guests had been off the terrace. The June rains that had been plaguing the area for a week had rendered the ground spongy. Though it was a clear night with filmy clouds flitting across a full moon, parts of the estate were stygian dark.

What impulse took him to the high point of the property about a quarter of a mile from the house where the old gazebo stood, he didn't know. It was as though another person guided his steps.

Pausing when he heard the murmur of voices, he took a deep breath and put back his head. He made the night sound he and his friends had used in Vietnam. Someone answered him from very close by.

"Where?" a voice in the dark whispered.

"Gazebo."

Con moved forward, all thought of being the head of a corporation fading away. His training in jungle warfare rose to the forefront of his mind, wrapping around him like a cloak.

Hearing Heller's voice threw him for a moment.

"Let Simeon go, John. I'll go with you, wherever you say, but I want the boy to go back to the house."

"I won't leave you, Mama."

"Stop the chatter." The shrill whisper cut through the darkness like a ragged scythe. "We're going now, or neither of you will leave here. Now, move."

Con faded back into the darkness, aware that Pacer and Dev were close at hand.

As they went past him, Heller first, then John with Simeon in front of him, his hand around the boy's neck, Con heard an infinitesimal sound. He moved immediately, grabbing for Heller and pulling her behind him as Pacer bent back the hand holding Simeon, then scooped the boy up under one arm.

Dev took John and almost broke his back when he slung him against a tree. "I should kill you, sucker," he said sweetly as he held John immobile with an arm against his throat. "You interfered with a child and my friend's wife. Tell me why I shouldn't throttle the life out of you."

"He can't answer you," Pacer drawled, "but he is turning a funny shade of blue. I think it's blue. In this light it's hard to tell."

"Don't kill him, Dev," Con said. "unless he moves.

Darling, are you all right?" He held Heller close, his hands traveling over her. "Simeon, come here."

"I'm fine," Heller said. She clung to Con with one arm, her other reaching out to the boy, who pressed his face against her. "Con, you would have been so proud of Simeon, he was so brave." She felt teary and weak as Simeon looked up at her and flashed a smile. All she wanted was to keep her son and her man close to her.

"Where do you want to question the crud, Rad?" Pacer asked. His normally placid features were harsh and unfriendly when he looked at John.

"Let's get him back to the library and alert the others that things are all right."

When Simon saw them enter the house and go into the library, he assessed the situation and began shepherding his wife and daughter out of the ballroom.

"There was something wrong, wasn't there, Simon?"

"Yes, my dear, but don't fret. Shh, Ione, don't ask any questions until we're safely in the library."

"Father, surely Heller couldn't have been in danger as mother inferred. Could she?"

"Con will explain everything, I'm sure." Simon urged the women into the library, then closed the double doors behind him.

Ione went to her husband, who took her in his arms, shushing her gently.

"Heller, are you all right?" Simon shot a quick glance at his son before he embraced his daughter-in-law. "You're trembling."

"I'm fine, sir. I—I was worried about Simeon."

"Simeon!" Melanie exclaimed. She hurried across

the room to the boy and clasped him close to her, tears in her eyes. "You are never to be out of Gramma's sight this summer, young man."

"Am I really staying here when Mama and Dad go on a trip?"

"Yes, indeed you are. Your cousins will be here and you shall do all manner of exciting things. Having your own horse will please you, I know."

"Horse?" Simeon's eyes rounded in wonder.

"Sorry, darling, I think Mother is trying to seduce him." Con kept his arm around Heller, as though if he released her she might disappear.

"She's succeeding admirably."

Heller smiled at Simeon, then gazed at the man who sat between Dev and Pacer on the sofa, his head bowed.

"Was it really his coveting of art that made him do the things he did?" she asked Con.

"Don't act so surprised. There are very sophisticated art thieves who take priceless masterpieces and make a very good living selling them to private collectors all over the world. The collectors never show them to anyone because, of course, they would be arrested immediately. Coveting great works of art and stealing them is an age-old pastime on this planet. For instance, during the Second World War Herman Goering was so greedy for the world's great art that he pillaged every country that Germany conquered, stealing magnificent masterpieces beloved by the nations that owned them."

"I knew about him, but it's still mind-boggling to imagine the desperation of such people." She shuddered and moved even closer to Con.

"Sit down, darling. You've been through quite a bit this evening."

"No, I'd rather be close to you." She turned to look up at him. "I love you, Con, and I won't let you go no matter how you wriggle."

"No fear of that," he told her huskily. He gazed lovingly at her, then realized someone was standing beside him, coughing to get his attention. Looking up, he was surprised to see the police had arrived. "Oh, sorry, Sergeant. I'll be right there." He looked back at Heller. "Don't move and don't change conversations. I'll join you in a moment. Damn, I'll be glad when we can be alone."

"Me too."

A little over a year later Heller was in the last weeks of her pregnancy, and Con was smothering his anxiety behind a rock-hard mask.

"Why's Rad so edgy?" Dev asked one night over after-dinner brandy.

"Daddy is nervous 'cause of the baby," Simeon said sagely, smiling at his beaming grandparents and his two "uncles." "Mama says he'll be better after it's over."

"He'd better be." Pacer laughed. "He couldn't be worse." He turned to Heller. "It was a delicious dinner, darlin', as usual."

"She runs this house beautifully," Melanie said proudly, smiling at her daughter-in-law.

Con entered the large living room of the apartment in Manhattan. Though they now had a house in Connecticut, they'd been staying here for two weeks so Con wouldn't be so far away from her when he went to work. He placed a pillow he'd fetched from their bedroom behind his wife.

"Con, I'm fine." Heller didn't know exactly how to

tell him that she'd been in labor for about two hours, so she decided to say nothing until it was absolutely necessary.

"My dear." Melanie sat down next to her and leaned toward her. "How long are the pains and how far apart?"

Heller smiled at the woman who was like her own mother. "I haven't actually timed them. Trust you to notice."

'I've been there. My advice is to just continue with the breathing you've been taught and bide your time. Have you told Con about the testing that showed two babies?"

"Not yet, but I will tonight."

"I think we'll take Simeon home with us tonight. We'll stay in our apartment here and get him to school in the morning. I'll call Doodie too."

"So you think it might be tonight, even though I'm not due for another week?"

Melanie nodded.

By the time the guests had left, taking a happily chattering Simeon with them, Heller was ready to call the doctor.

"You've been in pain, haven't you?" Con said. "I saw you talking to my mother."

"I honestly didn't think too much of it, but now I do." Heller was bemused and impressed at Conrad in action. Within minutes things were coordinated and they were on their way.

"But darling, it might not happen tonight," Heller protested as he bundled her into the hospital.

"I don't trust you. You have a habit of doing things rather speedily."

She caught her breath on a contraction but still laughed. "If you're talking about our lovemaking, I think I'm insulted."

"Stop joking, Heller. This isn't funny."

Three hours later a tired but happy Heller faced her pale husband. "Aren't they a surprise? I was going to tell you sooner, but things got in the way."

"When I told Simeon, he yelled so loud through the phone I think he shattered my eardrum. Our son has informed me that he likes being the oldest of three." Con gazed down at the babies. "A boy and a girl. God, Heller, they're so beautiful, and I love you so much."

"Lean down and kiss me. I need you, Con." When she saw tears well in his eyes, she reached up her arms. "You have made me so happy."

"And you brought me to life, angel."

"Will Dev and Pacer be coming to see the twins?"

"I doubt whether anyone will be able to keep them out of here. You have captivated them just as you have me."

"Oh, Con, we've come so far."

"And now we're a family." He kissed her tenderly. "Thank you, Heller Wendel."

THE EDITOR'S CORNER

What a wonderful summer of romance reading we have in store for you. Truly, you're going to be LOVESWEPT with some happy surprises through the long, hot, lazy days ahead.

First, you're going to get **POCKETS FULL OF JOY**, LOVESWEPT #270, by our new Canadian author, Judy Gill. Elaina McIvor wondered helplessly what she was going to do with an eleven-month-old baby to care for. Dr. "Brad" Bradshaw had been the stork and deposited the infant on her doorstep and raced away. But he was back soon enough to "play doctor" and "play house" in one of the most delightful and sensuous romances of the season.

Joan Elliott Pickart has created two of her most intriguing characters ever in **TATTERED WINGS**, LOVESWEPT #271. Devastatingly handsome Mark Hampton—an Air Force Colonel whose once exciting life now seems terribly lonely—and beautiful, enigmatic Eden Landry—a top fashion model who left her glamorous life for a secluded ranch—meet one snowy night. Desire flares immediately. But so do problems. Mark soon discovers that Eden is like a perfect butterfly encased in a cube of glass. You'll revel in the ways he finds to break down the walls without hurting the woman!

For all of you who've written to ask for Tara's and Jed's love story, here your fervent requests

(continued)

are answered with Barbara Boswell's terrific **AND TARA, TOO,** LOVESWEPT #272. As we know, Jed Ramsey is as darkly sleek and as seductive and as winning with women as a man can be. And Tara Brady wants no part of him. It would be just too convenient, she thinks, if all the Brady sisters married Ramsey men. But that's exactly what Jed's tyrannical father has in mind. You'll chuckle and gasp as Tara and Jed rattle the chains of fate in a breathlessly sensual and touching love story.

Margie McDonnell is an author who can transport you to another world. This time she takes you to **THE LAND OF ENCHANTMENT,** via LOVE-SWEPT #273, to meet a modern-day, ever so gallant knight, dashing Patrick Knight, and the sensitive and lovely Karen Harris. Karen is the single parent of an exceptional son and a quite sensible lady . . . until she falls for the handsome hunk who is as merry as he is creative. We think you'll delight in this very special, very thrilling love story.

It gives us enormous pleasure next month to celebrate the fifth anniversary of Iris Johansen's writing career. Her first ever published book was LOVESWEPT's **STORMY VOWS** in August 1983. With that and its companion romance **TEMPEST AT SEA,** published in September 1983, Iris launched the romance featuring spin-off and/or continuing characters. Now everyone's doing it! But, still,

(continued)

nobody does it quite like the woman who began it all, Iris Johansen. Here, next month, you'll meet old friends and new lovers in **BLUE SKIES AND SHINING PROMISES,** LOVESWEPT #274. (The following month she'll also have a LOVESWEPT, of course, and we wonder if you can guess who the featured characters will be.) Don't miss the thrilling love story of Cameron Bandor (yes, you know him) and Damita Shaughnessy, whose background will shock, surprise and move you, taking you right back to five years ago!

Welcome, back, Peggy Webb! In the utterly bewitching LOVESWEPT #275, **SLEEPLESS NIGHTS,** Peggy tells the story of Tanner Donovan of the quicksilver eyes and Amanda Lassiter of the tart tongue and tender heart. In this thrilling and sensuous story, you have a marvelous battle of wits between lovers parted in the past and determined to best each other in the present. A real delight!

As always, we hope that not one of our LOVE-SWEPTs will ever disappoint you. Enjoy!

Carolyn Nichols

Carolyn Nichols
　Editor
LOVESWEPT
Bantam Books
666 Fifth Avenue
New York, NY 10103

THE HOMETOWN HUNK CONTEST

FOR EVERY WOMAN WHO HAS EVER SAID—
"I know a man who looks
just like the hero of this book"
—**HAVE WE GOT A CONTEST FOR YOU!**

To help celebrate our fifth year of publishing LOVESWEPT we are having a fabulous, fun-filled event called THE HOMETOWN HUNK contest. We are going to reissue six classic early titles by six of your favorite authors.

DARLING OBSTACLES **by Barbara Boswell**
IN A CLASS BY ITSELF **by Sandra Brown**
C.J.'S FATE **by Kay Hooper**
THE LADY AND THE UNICORN **by Iris Johansen**
CHARADE **by Joan Elliott Pickart**
FOR THE LOVE OF SAMI **by Fayrene Preston**

Here, as in the backs of all July, August, and September 1988 LOVESWEPTS you will find "cover notes" just like the ones we prepare at Bantam as the background for our art director to create our covers. These notes will describe the hero and heroine, give a teaser on the plot, and suggest a scene for the cover. Your part in the contest will be to see if a great looking local man—or men, if your hometown is so blessed—fits our description of one of the heroes of the six books we will reissue.

THE HOMETOWN HUNK who is selected (one for each of the six titles) will be flown to New York via United Airlines and will stay at the Loews Summit Hotel—the ideal hotel for business or pleasure in midtown Manhattan—for two nights. All travel arrangements made by Reliable Travel International, Incorporated. He will be the model for the new cover of the book which will be released in mid-1989. The six people who send in the winning photos of their HOMETOWN HUNK will receive a pre-selected assortment of LOVESWEPT books free for one year. Please see the Official Rules above the Official Entry Form for full details and restrictions.

We can't wait to start judging those pictures! Oh, and you must let the man you've chosen know that you're entering him in the contest. After all, if he wins he'll have to come to New York.

Have fun. Here's your chance to get the cover-lover of your dreams!

Carolyn Nichols

Carolyn Nichols
Editor
LOVESWEPT
Bantam Books
666 Fifth Avenue
New York, NY 10102–0023

THE HOMETOWN HUNK CONTEST

DARLING OBSTACLES
(Originally Published as LOVESWEPT #95)
By Barbara Boswell

COVER NOTES

The Characters:

Hero:
GREG WILDER's gorgeous body and "to-die-for" good looks haven't hurt him in the dating department, but when most women discover he's a widower with four kids, they head for the hills! Greg has the hard, muscular build of an athlete, and his light brown hair, which he wears neatly parted on the side, is streaked blond by the sun. Add to that his aquamarine blue eyes that sparkle when he laughs, and his sensual mouth and generous lower lip, and you're probably wondering what woman in her right mind wouldn't want Greg's strong, capable surgeon's hands working their magic on her—kids or no kids!

Personality Traits:
An acclaimed neurosurgeon, Greg Wilder is a celebrity of sorts in the planned community of Woodland, Maryland. Authoritative, debonair, self-confident, his reputation for engaging in one casual relationship after another almost overshadows his prowess as a doctor. In reality, Greg dates more out of necessity than anything else, since he has to attend one social function after another. He considers most of the events boring and wishes he could spend more time with his children. But his profession is a difficult and demanding one—and being both father and mother to four kids isn't any less so. A thoughtful, generous, sometimes befuddled father, Greg tries to do it all. Cerebral, he uses his intellect and skill rather than physical strength to win his victories. However, he never expected to come up against one Mary Magdalene May!

Heroine:
MARY MAGDALENE MAY, called Maggie by her friends, is the thirty-two-year-old mother of three children. She has shoulder-length auburn hair, and green eyes that shout her Irish heritage. With high cheekbones and an upturned nose covered with a smattering of freckles, Maggie thinks of herself more as the girl-next-door type. Certainly, she believes, she could never be one of Greg Wilder's beautiful escorts.

Setting: The small town of Woodland, Maryland

The Story:
Surgeon Greg Wilder wanted to court the feisty and beautiful widow who'd been caring for his four kids, but she just wouldn't let him past her doorstep! Sure that his interest was only casual, and that he preferred more sophisticated women, Maggie May vowed to keep Greg at arm's length. But he wouldn't take no for an answer. And once he'd crashed through her defenses and pulled her into his arms, he was tireless—and reckless—in his campaign to win her over. Maggie had found it tough enough to resist one determined doctor; now he threatened to call in his kids and hers as reinforcements—seven rowdy snags to romance!

Cover scene:
As if romancing Maggie weren't hard enough, Greg can't seem to find time to spend with her without their children around. Stealing a private moment on the stairs in Maggie's house, Greg and Maggie embrace. She is standing one step above him, but she still has to look up at him to see into his eyes. Greg's hands are on her hips, and her hands are resting on his shoulders. Maggie is wearing a very sheer, short pink nightgown, and Greg has on wheat-colored jeans and a navy and yellow striped rugby shirt. Do they have time to kiss?

THE HOMETOWN HUNK CONTEST

IN A CLASS BY ITSELF
(Originally Published as LOVESWEPT #66)
By Sandra Brown

COVER NOTES

The Characters:

Hero:
LOGAN WEBSTER would have no trouble posing for a
Scandinavian travel poster. His wheat-colored hair always
seems to be tousled, defying attempts to control it, and
falls across his wide forehead. Thick eyebrows one shade
darker than his hair accentuate his crystal blue eyes. He
has a slender nose that flairs slightly over a mouth that
testifies to both sensitivity and strength. The faint lines
around his eyes and alongside his mouth give the impression that reaching the ripe age of 30 wasn't all fun and
games for him. Logan's square, determined jaw is punctu-
ated by a vertical cleft. His broad shoulders and narrow
waist add to his tall, lean appearance.

Personality traits:
Logan Webster has had to scrape and save and fight for
everything he's gotten. Born into a poor farm family, he
was driven to succeed and overcome his "wrong side of
the tracks" image. His businesses include cattle, real estate, and natural gas. Now a pillar of the community,
Logan's life has been a true rags-to-riches story. Only
Sandra Brown's own words can describe why he is masculinity epitomized: "Logan had 'the walk,' that saddle-
tramp saunter that was inherent to native Texan men,
passed down through generations of cowboys. It was, without even trying to be, sexy. The unconscious roll of the
hips, the slow strut, the flexed knees, the slouching stance,
the deceptive laziness that hid a latent aggressiveness."
Wow! And not only does he have "the walk," but he's fun

and generous and kind. Even with his wealth, he feels at home living in his small hometown with simple, hard-working, middle-class, backbone-of-America folks. A born leader, people automatically gravitate toward him.

Heroine:
DANI QUINN is a sophisticated twenty-eight-year-old woman. Dainty, her body compact, she is utterly feminine. Dani's pale, lustrous hair is moonlight and honey spun together, and because it is very straight, she usually wears it in a chignon. With golden eyes to match her golden hair, Dani is the one woman Logan hasn't been able to get off his mind for the ten years they've been apart.

Setting: Primarily on Logan's ranch in East Texas.

The Story:
Ten years had passed since Dani Quinn had graduated from high school in the small Texas town, ten years since the night her elopement with Logan Webster had ended in disaster. Now Dani approached her tenth reunion with uncertainty. Logan would be there . . . Logan, the only man who'd ever made her shiver with desire and need, but would she have the courage to face the fury in his eyes? She couldn't defend herself against his anger and hurt—to do so would demand she reveal the secret sorrow she shared with no one. Logan's touch had made her his so long ago. Could he reach past the pain to make her his for all time?

Cover Scene:
It's sunset, and Logan and Dani are standing beside the swimming pool on his ranch, embracing. The pool is surrounded by semitropical plants and lush flower beds. In the distance, acres of rolling pasture land resembling a green lake undulate into dense, piney woods. Dani is wearing a strapless, peacock blue bikini and sandals with leather ties that wrap around her ankles. Her hair is straight and loose, falling to the middle of her back. Logan has on a light-colored pair of corduroy shorts and a short-sleeved designer knit shirt in a pale shade of yellow.

THE HOMETOWN HUNK CONTEST

C.J.'S FATE
(Originally Published as LOVESWEPT #32)
By Kay Hooper

COVER NOTES

The Characters:

Hero:
FATE WESTON easily could have walked straight off an Indian reservation. His raven black hair and strong, well-molded features testify to his heritage. But somewhere along the line genetics threw Fate a curve—his eyes are the deepest, darkest blue imaginable! Above those blue eyes are dark slanted eyebrows, and fanning out from those eyes are faint laugh lines—the only sign of the fact that he's thirty-four years old. Tall, Fate moves with easy, loose-limbed grace. Although he isn't an athlete, Fate takes very good care of himself, and it shows in his strong physique. Striking at first glance and fascinating with each succeeding glance, the serious expressions on his face make him look older than his years, but with one smile he looks boyish again.

Personality traits:
Fate possesses a keen sense of humor. His heavy-lidded, intelligent eyes are capable of concealment, but there is a shrewdness in them that reveals the man hadn't needed college or a law degree to be considered intelligent. The set of his head tells you that he is proud—perhaps even a bit arrogant. He is attractive and perfectly well aware of that fact. Unconventional, paradoxical, tender, silly, lusty, gentle, comical, serious, absurd, and endearing are all words that come to mind when you think of Fate. He is not ashamed to be everything a man can be. A defense attorney by profession, one can detect a bit of frustrated actor in his character. More than anything else, though, it's the

impression of humor about him—reinforced by the elu
sive dimple in his cheek—that makes Fate Weston ;
scrumptious hero!

Heroine:
C.J. ADAMS is a twenty-six-year-old research librarian
Unaware of her own attractiveness, C.J. tends to play
down her pixylike figure and tawny gold eyes. But once
she meets Fate, she no longer feels that her short, bur
nished copper curls and the sprinkling of freckles on her
nose make her unappealing. He brings out the vixen in
her, and changes the smart, bookish woman who pro
fessed to have no interest in men into the beautiful, sexy
woman she really was all along. Now, if only he could get
her to tell him what C.J. stands for!

Setting: Ski lodge in Aspen, Colorado

The Story:
C.J. Adams had been teased enough about her seeming
lack of interest in the opposite sex. On a ski trip with her
five best friends, she impulsively embraced a handsome
stranger, pretending they were secret lovers—and the
delighted lawyer who joined in her impetuous charade
seized the moment to deepen the kiss. Astonished at his
reaction, C.J. tried to nip their romance in the bud—but
found herself nipping at his neck instead! She had met
her match in a man who could answer her witty remarks
with clever ripostes of his own, and a lover whose caresses
aroused in her a passionate need she'd never suspected
that she could feel. Had destiny somehow tossed them
together?

Cover Scene:
C.J. and Fate virtually have the ski slopes to themselves
early one morning, and they take advantage of it! Frolick-
ing in a snow drift, Fate is covering C.J. with snow—and
kisses! They are flushed from the cold weather and from
the excitement of being in love. C.J. is wearing a sky-blue,
one-piece, tight-fitting ski outfit that zips down the front.
Fate is wearing a navy blue parka and matching ski pants.

THE HOMETOWN HUNK CONTEST

THE LADY AND THE UNICORN
(Originally Published as LOVESWEPT #29)
By Iris Johansen

COVER NOTES

The Characters:

Hero:
Not classically handsome, RAFE SANTINE's blunt, craggy features reinforce the quality of overpowering virility about him. He has wide, Slavic cheekbones and a bold, thrusting chin, which give the impression of strength and authority. Thick black eyebrows are set over piercing dark eyes. He wears his heavy, dark hair long. His large frame measures in at almost six feet four inches, and it's hard to believe that a man with such brawny shoulders and strong thighs could exhibit the pantherlike grace which characterizes Rafe's movements. Rafe Santine is definitely a man to be reckoned with, and heroine Janna Cannon does just that!

Personality traits:
Our hero is a man who radiates an aura of power and danger, and women find him intriguing and irresistible. Rafe Santine is a self-made billionaire at the age of thirty-eight. Almost entirely self-educated, he left school at sixteen to work on his first construction job, and by the time he was twenty-three, he owned the company. From there he branched out into real estate, computers, and oil. Rafe reportedly changes mistresses as often as he changes shirts. His reputation for ruthless brilliance has been earned over years of fighting to the top of the economic ladder from the slums of New York. His gruff manner and hard personality hide the tender, vulnerable side of him. Rafe also possesses an insatiable thirst for knowledge that is a passion with him. Oddly enough, he has a wry sense of

humor that surfaces unexpectedly from time to time. And, though cynical to the extreme, he never lets his natural skepticism interfere with his innate sense of justice.

Heroine:

JANNA CANNON, a game warden for a small wildlife preserve, is a very dedicated lady. She is tall at five feet nine inches and carries herself in a stately way. Her long hair is dark brown and is usually twisted into a single thick braid in back. Of course, Rafe never lets her keep her hair braided when they make love! Janna is one quarter Cherokee Indian by heritage, and she possesses the dark eyes and skin of her ancestors.

Setting: Rafe's estate in Carmel, California

The Story:

Janna Cannon scaled the high walls of Rafe Santine's private estate, afraid of nothing and determined to appeal to the powerful man who could save her beloved animal preserve. She bewitched his guard dogs, then cast a spell of enchantment over him as well. Janna's profound grace, her caring nature, made the tough and proud Rafe grow mercurial in her presence. She offered him a gift he'd never risked reaching out for before—but could he trust his own emotions enough to open himself to her love?

Cover Scene:

In the gazebo overlooking the rugged cliffs at the edge of the Pacific Ocean, Rafe and Janna share a passionate moment together. The gazebo is made of redwood and the interior is small and cozy. Scarlet cushions cover the benches, and matching scarlet curtains hang from the eaves, caught back by tasseled sashes to permit the sea breeze to whip through the enclosure. Rafe is wearing black suede pants and a charcoal gray crew-neck sweater. Janna is wearing a safari-style khaki shirt-and-slacks outfit and suede desert boots. They embrace against the breathtaking backdrop of wild, crashing, white-crested waves pounding the rocks and cliffs below.

THE HOMETOWN HUNK CONTEST

CHARADE
(Originally Published as LOVESWEPT #74)
By Joan Elliott Pickart

COVER NOTES

The Characters:

Hero:
The phrase tall, dark, and handsome was coined to describe TENNES WHITNEY. His coal black hair reaches
past his collar in back, and his fathomless steel gray eyes
are framed by the kind of thick, dark lashes that a woman
would kill to have. Darkly tanned, Tennes has a straight
nose and a square chin, with—you guessed it!—a Kirk
Douglas cleft. Tennes oozes masculinity and virility. He's
a handsome son-of-a-gun!

Personality traits:
A shrewd, ruthless business tycoon, Tennes is a man of
strength and principle. He's perfected the art of buying
floundering companies and turning them around finan-
cially, then selling them at a profit. He possesses a sixth
sense about business—in short, he's a winner! But there
are two sides to his personality. Always in cool command,
Tennes, who fears no man or challenge, is rendered emotionally vulnerable when faced with his elderly aunt's illness. His deep devotion to the woman who raised him
clearly casts him as a warm, compassionate guy—not at
all like the tough-as-nails executive image he presents.
Leave it to heroine Whitney Jordan to discover the real
man behind the complicated enigma.

Heroine:
WHITNEY JORDAN's russet-colored hair floats past her
shoulders in glorious waves. Her emerald green eyes, full
breasts, and long, slender legs—not to mention her peaches-

and-cream complexion—make her eye-poppingly attractive. How can Tennes resist the twenty-six-year-old beauty? And how can Whitney consider becoming serious with him? If their romance flourishes, she may end up being Whitney Whitney!

Setting: Los Angeles, California

The Story:
One moment writer Whitney Jordan was strolling the aisles of McNeil's Department Store, plotting the untimely demise of a soap opera heartthrob; the next, she was nearly knocked over by a real-life stunner who implored her to be his fiancée! The ailing little gray-haired aunt who'd raised him had one final wish, he said—to see her dear nephew Tennes married to the wonderful girl he'd described in his letters . . . only that girl hadn't existed—until now! Tennes promised the masquerade would last only through lunch, but Whitney gave such an inspired performance that Aunt Olive refused to let her go. And what began as a playful romantic deception grew more breathlessly real by the minute. . . .

Cover Scene:
Whitney's living room is bright and cheerful. The gray carpeting and blue sofa with green and blue throw pillows gives the apartment a cool but welcoming appearance. Sitting on the sofa next to Tennes, Whitney is wearing a black crepe dress that is simply cut but stunning. It is cut low over her breasts and held at the shoulders by thin straps. The skirt falls to her knees in soft folds and the bodice is nipped in at the waist with a matching belt. She has on black high heels, but prefers not to wear any jewelry to spoil the simplicity of the dress. Tennes is dressed in a black suit with a white silk shirt and a deep red tie.

THE HOMETOWN HUNK CONTEST

FOR THE LOVE OF SAMI
(Originally Published as LOVESWEPT #34)
By Fayrene Preston

COVER NOTES

Hero:
DANIEL PARKER-ST. JAMES is every woman's dream come true. With glossy black hair and warm, reassuring blue eyes, he makes our heroine melt with just a glance. Daniel's lean face is chiseled into assertive planes. His lips are full and firmly sculptured, and his chin has the determined and arrogant thrust to it only a man who's sure of himself can carry off. Daniel has a lot in common with Clark Kent. Both wear glasses, and when Daniel removes them to make love to Sami, she thinks he really is Superman!

Personality traits:
Daniel Parker-St. James is one of the Twin Cities' most respected attorneys. He's always in the news, either in the society columns with his latest society lady, or on the front page with his headline cases. He's brilliant and takes on only the toughest cases—usually those that involve millions of dollars. Daniel has a reputation for being a deadly opponent in the courtroom. Because he's from a socially prominent family and is a Harvard graduate, it's expected that he'll run for the Senate one day. Distinguished-looking and always distinctively dressed—he's fastidious about his appearance—Daniel gives off an unassailable air of authority and absolute control.

Heroine:
SAMUELINA (SAMI) ADKINSON is secretly a wealthy heiress. No one would guess. She lives in a converted warehouse loft, dresses to suit no one but herself, and dabbles in the creative arts. Sami is twenty-six years old, with

long, honey-colored hair. She wears soft, wispy bangs and has very thick brown lashes framing her golden eyes. Of medium height, Sami has to look up to gaze into Daniel's deep blue eyes.

Setting: St. Paul, Minnesota

The Story:
Unpredictable heiress Sami Adkinson had endeared herself to the most surprising people—from the bag ladies in the park she protected . . . to the mobster who appointed himself her guardian . . . to her exasperated but loving friends. Then Sami was arrested while demonstrating to save baby seals, and it took powerful attorney Daniel Parker-St. James to bail her out. Daniel was smitten, soon cherishing Sami and protecting her from her night fears. Sami reveled in his love—and resisted it too. And holding on to Sami, Daniel discovered, was like trying to hug quicksilver. . . .

Cover Scene:
The interior of Daniel's house is very grand and supremely formal, the decor sophisticated, refined, and quietly tasteful, just like Daniel himself. Rich traditional fabrics cover plush oversized custom sofas and Regency wing chairs. Queen Anne furniture is mixed with Chippendale and is subtly complemented with Oriental accent pieces. In the library, floor-to-ceiling bookcases filled with rare books provide the backdrop for Sami and Daniel's embrace. Sami is wearing a gold satin sheath gown. The dress has a high neckline, but in back is cut provocatively to the waist. Her jewels are exquisite. The necklace is made up of clusters of flowers created by large, flawless diamonds. From every cluster a huge, perfectly matched teardrop emerald hangs. The earrings are composed of an even larger flower cluster, and an equally huge teardrop-shaped emerald hangs from each one. Daniel is wearing a classic, elegant tuxedo.

LOVESWEPT® HOMETOWN HUNK CONTEST

OFFICIAL RULES

> IN A CLASS BY ITSELF by Sandra Brown
> FOR THE LOVE OF SAMI by Fayrene Preston
> C.J.'S FATE by Kay Hooper
> THE LADY AND THE UNICORN by Iris Johansen
> CHARADE by Joan Elliott Pickart
> DARLING OBSTACLES by Barbara Boswell

1. NO PURCHASE NECESSARY. Enter the HOMETOWN HUNK contest by completing the Official Entry Form below and enclosing a sharp color full-length photograph (easy to see details, with the photo being no smaller than 2½" × 3½") of the man you think perfectly represents one of the heroes from the above-listed books which are described in the accompanying Loveswept cover notes. Please be sure to fill out the Official Entry Form completely, and also be sure to clearly print on the back of the man's photograph the man's name, address, city, state, zip code, telephone number, date of birth, your name, address, city, state, zip code, telephone number, your relationship, if any, to the man (e.g. wife, girlfriend) as well as the title of the Loveswept book for which you are entering the man. If you do not have an Official Entry Form, you can print all of the required information on a 3" × 5" card and attach it to the photograph with all the necessary information printed on the back of the photograph as well. YOUR HERO MUST SIGN BOTH THE BACK OF THE OFFICIAL ENTRY FORM (OR 3" × 5" CARD) AND THE PHOTOGRAPH TO SIGNIFY HIS CONSENT TO BEING ENTERED IN THE CONTEST. Completed entries should be sent to:

> BANTAM BOOKS
> HOMETOWN HUNK CONTEST
> Department CN
> 666 Fifth Avenue
> New York, New York 10102–0023

All photographs and entries become the property of Bantam Books and will not be returned under any circumstances.

2. Six men will be chosen by the Loveswept authors as a HOMETOWN HUNK (one HUNK per Loveswept title). By entering the contest, each winner and each person who enters a winner agrees to abide by Bantam Books' rules and to be subject to Bantam Books' eligibility requirements. Each winning HUNK and each person who enters a winner will be required to sign all papers deemed necessary by Bantam Books before receiving any prize. Each winning HUNK will be flown via **United Airlines** from his closest United Airlines-serviced city to New York City and will stay at the ⊔⊔ S⊔⊔⊔⊔⊔ Hotel—the ideal hotel for business or pleasure in midtown Manhattan— for two nights. Winning HUNKS' meals and hotel transfers will be provided by Bantam Books. Travel and hotel arrangements are made by *RELIABLE TRAVEL* and are subject to availability and to Bantam Books' date requirements. Each winning HUNK will pose with a female model at a photographer's studio for a photograph that will serve as the basis of a Loveswept front cover. Each winning HUNK will receive a $150.00 modeling fee. Each winning HUNK will be required to sign an Affidavit of Eligibility and Model's Release supplied by Bantam Books. (Approximate retail value of HOMETOWN HUNK'S PRIZE: $900.00). The six people who send in a winning HOMETOWN HUNK photograph that is used by Bantam will receive free for one year each, LOVESWEPT romance paperback books published by Bantam during that year. (Approximate retail value: $180.00.) Each person who submits a winning photograph

will also be required to sign an Affidavit of Eligibility and Promotional Release supplied by Bantam Books. All winning HUNKS' (as well as the people who submit the winning photographs) names, addresses, biographical data and likenesses may be used by Bantam Books for publicity and promotional purposes without any additional compensation. There will be no prize substitutions or cash equivalents made.

3. All completed entries must be received by Bantam Books no later than September 15, 1988. Bantam Books is not responsible for lost or misdirected entries. The finalists will be selected by Loveswept editors and the six winning HOMETOWN HUNKS will be selected by the six authors of the participating Loveswept books. Winners will be selected on the basis of how closely the judges believe they reflect the descriptions of the books' heroes. Winners will be notified on or about October 31, 1988. If there are insufficient entries or if in the judges' opinions, no entry is suitable or adequately reflects the descriptions of the hero(s) in the book(s), Bantam may decide not to award a prize for the applicable book(s) and may reissue the book(s) at its discretion.

4. The contest is open to residents of the U.S. and Canada, except the Province of Quebec, and is void where prohibited by law. All federal and local regulations apply. Employees of Reliable Travel International, Inc., United Airlines, the Summit Hotel, and the Bantam Doubleday Dell Publishing Group, Inc., their subsidiaries and affiliates, and their immediate families are ineligible to enter.

5. For an extra copy of the Official Rules, the Official Entry Form, and the accompanying Loveswept cover notes, send your request and a self-addressed stamped envelope (Vermont and Washington State residents need not affix postage) before August 20, 1988 to the address listed in Paragraph 1 above.

LOVESWEPT® HOMETOWN HUNK OFFICIAL ENTRY FORM

BANTAM BOOKS
HOMETOWN HUNK CONTEST
Dept. CN
666 Fifth Avenue
New York, New York 10102–0023

HOMETOWN HUNK CONTEST

YOUR NAME_____

YOUR ADDRESS_____

CITY_____ STATE_____ ZIP_____

THE NAME OF THE LOVESWEPT BOOK FOR WHICH YOU ARE ENTERING THIS PHOTO

_____by_____

YOUR RELATIONSHIP TO YOUR HERO_____

YOUR HERO'S NAME_____

YOUR HERO'S ADDRESS_____

CITY_____ STATE_____ ZIP_____

YOUR HERO'S TELEPHONE #_____

YOUR HERO'S DATE OF BIRTH_____

YOUR HERO'S SIGNATURE CONSENTING TO HIS PHOTOGRAPH ENTRY

_____